KJ MOORE

DOLLS

BLOOD BOUND BOOKS

Copyright © 2012 by KJ Moore
All rights reserved

ISBN 978-0-9849782-2-9

This book is a work of fiction. Names, characters, business organizations, places, events and incidents either are the product of the author's imagination or are used fictitiously. Any resemblance to actual persons, living or dead, events or locales is entirely coincidental.

Artwork by Lauren Shannon

Printed in the United States of America

First Edition

Visit us on the web at:
www.bloodboundbooks.net

Anthologies Available from Blood Bound Books:

Night Terrors II

Rock 'N' Roll is Dead: Dark Tales Inspired by Music

Night Terrors: An Anthology of Horror

Unspeakable: A New Breed of Terror

D.O.A.: Extreme Horror Collection

Seasons in the Abyss: Flash Fiction Anthology

Steamy Screams: Erotic Horror Anthology

Novels & Novellas:

Scarecrow & The Madness by Craig Saunders & Robert Essig

Monster Porn by KJ Moore

Feeding Ambition by Lawrence Conquest

At the End of All Things by Stony Graves

The Sinner by K. Trap Jones

Sons of the Pope by Daniel O' Connor

For all those in weird niches and wonderful sub-communities who are unapologetic in their happiness.

Chapter 1

Valley of the Dolls

It's a night for orange lightning out here in the desert. The storm has been going for hours, and we have been lashing through the rain at insane speeds in a leaking car. The only comfort has been the unwaveringly straight road and the knowledge that, on a night like this, any cop who sees a speeding nutter is going to leave them well enough alone. Sitting in a patrol car flicking peanuts and pretzels onto the dash, watching the salt get stuck on electrical tape hoarded from a discovered sex crime victim, they might see the streak of us fly past. Then, the most attention they'd give us is to wait for the distant sound of an impact and seek us out to masturbate over our torn remains. Or maybe not. The odds of us hitting anything are pretty slim. I'm pretty sure that, aside from the shack we're headed to, there's little else to really smash into out here.

The shack isn't in a much better state than the car when we finally reach it: an island of warped wood amidst slanting, dead grass with a disused gas station a few miles away. Hugh is our little contact in this area, a man seriously underweight because he still cuts his cocaine with laxatives. Hugh got into the laxatives when his dealer started doing it on the quiet, and when Hugh found out and decided that he liked it, he just kept it up. Hugh lives with his slave Nora, though not in the Black or Gorean way. In their contract, there's no infallible knowledge of the books of Gor, nor strict adherence to the slave positions.

It's just good, clean Domination slavery. She cooks, cleans and performs oral sex on command, and, in return, Hugh has never laid eyes in a desirous manner on another woman and showers her with praise and adoration.

I'm greatly envious of their commitment to one another. If I had a girl so hopelessly in love with me that she'd offer her mind as well as her body and heart like Nora does, I wouldn't know what to do with it. Nora has worn her high leather collar for five years now, exactly the same amount of time as her wedding ring. I can't make a commitment like that to one brand of whiskey, let alone a human being. They're a right honourable couple, and the fetish scene is friendly to them as such. Thus, they're in and privy to all the talk and gossip.

Tilley and I took ourselves on this mad venture into the domestically blissful land of their haven to be detectives, or at least to have something to do on an otherwise empty and wasted week. We didn't exactly fill the car with alcohol, but the dashboard is rammed and has to be taped shut. I never much saw the point of stashing bottles in the boot. No way to get to them in an emergency. The tape isn't exactly convenient for that, but I've got Tilley and her craft knife to attend to that when I need a drink quick. I'm way too paranoid to keep the bottles out in the open. I can just picture coming back to the car and seeing one of those birds, the ones that drop tortoises from hundreds and hundreds of feet down onto rocks to smash their shells, making off with a bottle of pure pot still whiskey, imported and worth more than I'd price Tilley. I'd have chased that bird across the Earth for destroying a bottle of Redbreast, and then roasted its body over its own nest, using its own fluffy chicks as kindling.

The engine's off and Tilley doesn't say anything as I sit in the car and finish running through this monologue to myself, muttering the occasional odd word around an unlit cigarette. After a few minutes she takes a nail file from the car-mat and starts blunting off her nails until they're all square-ended. I end up just watching her do that and when she's done, I open the door and start letting the rain in. Shoving the door shut and ducking into my collar, I jog to the house. Tilley follows at a far more leisurely pace, lifting her ankles high about the deepest wells in the mud.

I knock hard and let us both in when I hear a rumbled response, not knowing if it's an invitation or not, and not much caring. Nora comes out of the kitchen in a fake snake-skin top with corners that pull down into suspenders; the suspenders hold up wrecked fishnet stockings. Her boots are polished mirrors and have lines of studded corset lacing up the fronts and backs. A metal yoke is across her shoulders, her fine wrists held out by supple leather cuffs with a red velvet trim. I admire the craftsmanship from inside the doorway.

"Sir is in the living area," Nora tells us, her softly smiling face perfect and glowing. Hugh buys her enough moisturiser to submerge herself in every year, and rubs it with long, loving strokes into her skin. I've seen him do it.

"Thanks, Nora," Tilley says from behind me, sliding off her leather duster and hanging it on the hat rack.

Nora smiles again, looking younger than she is and trots delicately back into the kitchen. I take hold of Tilley's wrist and lead her through the hallway and into the living room, wincing at the '70s style wallpaper and the sickly carpet, swirled with flat and faded patterns. Hugh has always been firm on his priorities when it comes to spending money earned from doing…whatever. First come the drugs, food, then the toys and accessories. The shack can keep sinking into the mud until the occasional downpours start to damage those first items.

In the living room, there isn't a sofa pointed at the television. Instead, Hugh is reclining half-drunk in his bed-nest of sex dolls, all under-inflated and shining from their orifices. They squeak against each other when he fidgets around and when, after squintingly identifying us, he climbs to his feet.

I shake his hand and clap his shoulder with the usual grunted greeting, still staring at the dolls. To my knowledge, he doesn't actually penetrate them. He's got an adored slave for that. Mostly he knocks them around, sometimes two at a time, and cleans them up in the bath afterwards, making them warm. Any man who takes such copious amounts of drugs invariably has a dark side lurking far too close to the surface. When it comes up, Nora shuts herself off in the kitchen to bake cookies and lets him beat on the dolls, swearing indiscriminatingly. Later he'll beat on her, but she'll enjoy that and have the assurance of him actually listening to her safe word.

Tilley shakes his hand next and then goes to perch on the edge of the grey armchair in the corner of the room. I sit on the arm of it, running a hand down through her tangerine hair before propping my elbow on my knee. Hugh offers us drinks, which we gladly accept, and arranges the dolls again, slotting heads between dimpled thighs to make a sturdier platform on which to sit: like some weird futon.

I speak before Tilley can. "I heard that Carl's boyfriend died last week. Suffocated in a gimp suit."

No one laughs, though it is so tragically funny that we all want to. Hugh's bottom lip comes out bitten grey. "Yeah, I heard. Nasty thing. Zip got jammed or something. Not too sure. Carl's really torn up about it. Dominique is setting up a charity thing for the funeral."

Dominique is a female name meaning "of the lord." Dominique is a post-op transsexual who custom makes rubber-wear and will likely hold an auction of some of her clothing for this "charity thing." It wasn't one of her hoods that Ben turned blue in, I don't think.

I take the cigarette that's still sitting lonesome and cool from between my lips, thinking about sticking it behind my ear but deciding against it when I feel how wet my hair is. I give it to Tilley instead. She doesn't light it, just plays it in her hands, flipping it up and down along her fingers.

Nora comes in with a tray expertly held in her left hand, the drinks a meter from her head. She kneels so we can take them—fresh lemonade with a shot of vodka in each—and does the same for her husband, smiling demurely in her yoke. She offers us coke and cookies, but we all decline, and Hugh pats her arse lovingly when she makes her way back out.

"So, you came all the way out here just for the lemonade, or is there something else?" Hugh asks us after we all take long, refreshing sips from the tall glasses.

I sit back on the wide, bony arm. "It just all sounds really…"

"Suspicious," Tilley finishes, her lower lip against the rim of her glass.

Hugh looks interested, running a finger idly around the deep mouth of one of the dolls. I continue: "No one's saying if it was actually Carl that Ben was sceneing with. I don't know if Carl liked to share his gimp with other Doms."

"You think that maybe one of the Doms plugged Ben's air-hole and murdered him?"

"Well, it's not outside the realms of possibility now, is it? I mean, the cops weren't gonna perform an inquiry into the fetish scene, were they? So some freaky guy with a neo-Nazi boyfriend who had an extensive collection of ball, bit and ring gags died performing some "obscene" sex act. Who in vanilla society gives a shit?"

"I take your point," Hugh mutters eventually, finishing his lemonade and roughly shoving the base of the glass into a doll's mouth so it doesn't tip and spill its grainy dregs onto the appalling carpet. "So what do you want to do? Start asking questions in the scene about where Ben was in the last few days? Interrogate someone for real under the guise of a session?"

"Tilley can break a cane across a guy," I offer, seeing that as a helpful bit of information right then.

Hugh doesn't find that funny and pulls a face. "Oh yeah, all that is really going to inspire trust, isn't it? Seriously, mate, you sound like a fucking lunatic sometimes."

"Full moon," I reply with a grin. "I'm not saying we should pin anyone down and lick their eyes until they talk. You could just send out some feelers; keep your ear to the ground whilst Tilley and I do some more direct sniffing around."

The glass comes out of the sex doll's mouth with a flat pop and Hugh tips it upside down to let the dregs slide down, licking them off the rim when they reach the bottom. He wipes his mouth and nods to us. "Alright, I'll call you with anything I find out."

"We'll do the same." I stand up and neck the last of the lemonade, handing the glass down to Tilley. "Cheers mate. It's all I wanted."

Tilley utters a thank you as well and carries our glasses out to Nora, taking Hugh's from him on the way out. When Hugh gets up, the sex dolls groan out a farting sound like a mysteriously sentient rubber duck trying not to have diarrhea all over itself. He and I hang about in comfortable silence until Tilley gets back and then we both make our way to the door.

Nora tips one suspended arm and her head around the kitchen door whilst Tilley puts her heavy coat back on. "Safe ride back," she chirps. "It's gotten heavier out there."

I give her a little wave of thanks and take my cigarette back off Tilley, opening the door for us both and making a dash for the car, the cigarette hidden up my sleeve to stay dry. The ground is still in shock from the rain, which is hammering down in wide sheets. The top soil is floating like iron filings on the shuddering puddles, and I see it has left rings of dirt around Tilley's boots when she gets into the car.

Finally, I light the cigarette with a cheap blue lighter that had been pushed into a broken air vent, and fill the car with smoke within a few hard-puffing minutes. When I'm assured that the nicotine is safely in my blood, I start the engine and we drive off. Tilley peels open a crumpled map and starts drawing a line with her finger to a motel, murmuring instructions—just loud enough to be heard over the engine—to go north. I'm trying to deal with a potential murder here. I don't need her voice rattling my nerves.

Chapter 2
—
Next

Five hours later the sun's up and I'm tired through to the marrow. We pull under the overhang of a hotel and get a ticket stub, spending a few minutes picking open the dash cupboard to pour the contents into Tilley's bag. A few minutes later, we're making our way through the lobby of our rest stop for tonight.

The room is about what I'd expected for the money. The carpet is cheap and artificially shaggy, with long loops of fabric that would hold water well if I chose to flood the bathroom and wade around. We're not going to be here long enough to really make use of that though, so I don't bother.

Tilley stands over the sink and trims her fringe with nail scissors, clumped strands of hair drifting down into the basin below. I unwrap the tiny bars of soap and throw the wrappers in the bin whilst sitting on the lid of the toilet, watching her, following the sloping curves of her body. She's built for comfort, whereas I'm built for speed. I don't mean to say she's fat there, quite the contrary: she's got the lithe look of a swimsuit model. I can just see her as the type to settle down one day and have a black lab. I, on the other hand, would be lucky to get a loan from a bank big enough to cover the initial expenses of a house, by which I mean the liquor cabinet.

Sitting on the toilet, I realise that I don't really know what I'm doing. We've only got a week, I've got no real leads after the first day, and I'm not too sure how to proceed on the road to solving Ben's death. That is, of course, assuming that Ben was murdered and that this wasn't the result of a tragic sadomasochistic accident. Those do happen.

I can't tell Tilley of my wavering confidence in this mission, though. She's far too invested in the investigation, though I may be confusing that with an investment in me. Our relationship is a blurry thing in terms of definition, which is just the way I like it.

I go into the other room to get my journal, returning to the toilet to write that down. I like to keep a record of these clearer and more profound thoughts for the sake of deeming myself to be a philosophical genius on the topic of my own life when re-reading whilst drunk. I used to keep an online journal. It wasn't a popular blog until suddenly, one entry was.

I was twenty and in the final stages of moving out of my parent's house. I'd come home to use the internet and found my family in various positions of bloody death all over the living room. My blog entry read:

My family is dead. I don't know what to do or who to call. Obviously the police, but I accidentally threw up on Mum's head and I feel I ought to clean that up before they come. I can't touch her yet though. She's still warm and her skin is still supple. I'm going to wait for her to go cold first before I clean her face. I also want to find out what else is missing so I can make an orderly list.

I want to call Laura, but that's stupid. It wouldn't be fair to bring her over just for the sake of having her hold my hand whilst the coroners and police go over the place. She could help me with the dogs though. They're not dead, just shot in the legs. They'll probably be alright if they see a vet, but I'd have to call out a vet because I'm on the bike and I can't take them myself. And if someone came to drive us then I'd have to explain why I haven't called the police yet about the bodies, which would make me feel small and stupid. Laura wouldn't ask those kinds of questions at first though, and Laura has a car.

I went on to ramble some crap about the wireless and when I was going to find time to transfer the money and the bills and everything. Laura was my ex-girlfriend and the longest sane relationship of my life. The entry got read out in court some time later, which did nothing to inspire her to come back to me. It was horrible listening to my inane, heartless words. Some people thought it was me, and after hearing that out loud I wasn't all that surprised. It all blew over, however, and the right guys went down and all that.

Having the country riveted on my words though, my diatribe written in shock, gave me the bug. I needed people to read my words more, so I got into the writing gig. But I don't keep a blog anymore. I probably shouldn't keep a paper journal either, but I don't write in it nearly as often or in as much detail, so it doesn't matter all that much. Still, there's enough in there to warrant hiding it away in locked rooms.

I'm only documenting titbits about this investigation. I'd followed up my earlier notion of calling in on the munches and clubs local to Ben's area, but a few phone calls had confirmed to me that he didn't attend any of them regularly. Midway through the referred-onwards calls I realised that it wasn't a reliable enough track to pursue for testimonies anyway. Hearsay is all well and good, but not in the way that solid evidence for an investigation should be. We needed eyewitnesses, people who had met Ben and his partners, gotten to know his quirks and interests. People who knew if he liked wearing a hood.

Thus, there was no point in driving to these places. A list of suspects was next on the obviousness agenda, but that was a prickly one too. If he wasn't seen with someone often, then likely people wouldn't know who he was or the name of the men he was regularly with. We're only a few hours from Ben's home turf, though, so there's no harm in snooping around and seeing what we can find. I follow on this train of thought until Tilley finishes cutting her hair.

She leans back to inspect it, scrunching up her nose and sticking out her lip to blow air up her forehead. She's still scrutinising when she speaks to me for the first time in an hour. "Ben wasn't an American, you know. He was only over here on a work visa."

It's like she's fucking psychic. I dump my journal on the side of the bath with a hearty slapping sound. She's just gone and blown a huge hole in the only real direction I had in mind to take this investigation next, lumping us both firmly back at square one unless Hugh hears something and calls us inside the next twenty hours.

I suck and pull at the saliva glands under my tongue, mulling and grousing alternately. If he's not been here long then he wouldn't be established within the scene, in his peripheral way, to be known to anyone. There's practically no point in even trying to seek interviewees. That left the hood: the only solid thing about this whole case. We'd have to find the seller who'd sold Ben his gimp hood. It was an older model though, so if he'd only been in the country for a few years, he would have brought it with him. "Well where the hell is he from?"

"England," Tilley tells me smartly, fluffing her fringe before putting the tiny scissors down. "Cotswolds. The green, pricey bit. I think he'd only been over here about a year."

"Well that's just marvellous," I grouse back, slumping. "How the hell did you find that out?"

"I got his mum's number," Tilley replies around the sewing needle from the complimentary kit that she's using to slide out bits of food from between the gaps in her teeth. "She's still in England, and his body's getting taken back for the funeral. We're not invited to the wake."

I sit back, quietly and bitterly impressed. It's quite clear to me now that this investigation is going to take more than a week. It doesn't upset me as much as I thought it would though. I could use a holiday, even a working one. "Want to go to England?"

"Can you afford it?" She looks at me finally, genuinely curious about my financial status.

She knows I write but she doesn't know what and probably wouldn't read it anyway. I write under another name because I won't get hounded at my home for my books that way. The dust jacket photos were a stupid idea really, but I'm too much of an egotistical bastard not to. So it's just the false name and dark corners of the world that saves me. My last reasonable seller was a book about female castration with a narrative stapled to it. It wasn't a hard book to write. Make friends with the women of an Egyptian village, pretend you have a local pre-teen daughter, and they'll let you sit in the room and listen whilst they dig her clitoris out. I wrote the book in a week and a half. The sales preyed successfully on the morbid curiosity of the general public, and I have been largely living off those cheques for the last year.

I don't let any of this show up on my face when I answer Tilley. She has a phenomenal ability to read faces, particularly mine, so I get away with dick around her. "Yeah. Nothing fancy, but we can go for a while."

"You know, we could just go see Carl and gauge what he says."

Her logic offends me. "And where's the bloody fun in that? Let's draw this out a bit and have some fun."

Chapter 3

Republican Flogging

On the plane, Tilley holds my wrist with pale joints until we're high and level in the sky. Then she somehow finds the relaxed composure to turn off her overhead light and go to sleep, curled up sideways against the curve of the cabin. It's like she's got a gland somewhere that releases organic sedatives throughout her body when she squeezes it, sending her from white-knuckle anxiety to slumber that a baby would envy. If I could bottle that gland, I'd eat a drop of it to see what it'd do and sell the rest. Pure adrenaline taken from a living gland is so potent that you use an eyedropper or a Q-tip to suck it from. The human body already has a drug for every recreational drug we've put the time and effort into making ourselves. Let's have some pure endorphin drops, chewable testosterone and blotter paper sticky with brain juice. Let's get rich, quite literally, off our own backs.

This cheap flight has no complimentary peanuts so I hand over the inordinate cost of a bag and tear into them with vigour. On the tray table, I lay out the newspaper I bought at the airport and start jotting notes of how we should proceed when we get to England. I'm able to concentrate on this for about five minutes before my mind, inevitably, wanders.

My first kick-in-the-nuts taste of fetish was four years ago, when Hugh called me in the middle of the night and summoned me down to Neuro, the only decent pub for miles where you can scratch pink sawdust out from the corners with your nails. I'd been in the middle of redrafting a manuscript that my agent had wanted a week before. He was an exceptional case of crazy and phoned me daily whilst taking a shit to hurl new and unprintable insults at me, demanding his book. Of course, this just made me want to piss the guy off more, so after sending a package marked Manuscript filled with dead lizards, I settled to taking my sweet time with it.

So, when Hugh called me saying that something highly suited to my brand of mind was going on, I was out the door without hesitation. It was a short drive to Neuro but I burned through four cigarettes from my dashboard stash to wake up. Scott the barman, body of a troll and demeanour of a randy terrier, sent me down to the basement bar, which was a promising start.

* * *

I hear the jeers and the crack of leather before I get all the way down the stairs. A scrawny ginger bastard I've never seen before is duct-taped to the security rails that had been pulled down at one end of the bar, a guy serving pints past him with an outright smirk. Ginger Boy's long hair is tied into an erect plume at the top of his head, a ball gag glistening between his teeth and he's topless. The punters had written all over his torso with permanent black marker: coloured in nipples; an arrow with the words Little One down his stomach and another arrow with Cock Here down his back, among other things. Mercifully he's blindfolded too, so he can't see the complete strangers like me taking photos and videos of him being flogged by a pink-haired girl with their phones. Two guys shove past me to go back upstairs as they were talking downloads.

Hugh sees me from a table at the back and waves me over, Nora corseted and looking radiant next to him. He's already gotten me a whiskey mixer, a double because he doesn't believe in singles.

"How're you doing, you bastard?" he yells when I get near to him. Clearly off his tits, I figure if I thought to suck his armpit I'd immediately overdose on any number of things. He gestures wildly at the scene. It seems it's not just the pink girl inflicting pain on the lad—implements are being passed around freely. "So what do you reckon?"

I take a drink and another appraising look. "Well, it's one of the more fucked up things I've seen on a small scale recently. Any occasion?"

"It's that lad's birthday," Hugh informs, jabbing with an unlit roll-up at the gagged victim. Nora produces a lighter from deep within her full, tight cleavage. "Sod's lucky it's just this happening. Scott wanted to get him in a truck, strip him naked, and leave him out on the interstate with a billboard saying Fuck the Blacks." Sounds like something Scott would do to anyone on any old day. "Look at him though. Having the time of his life."

I tip my head to a right angle, watching him trying to scream around the rubber gag as red stripes build up on his body. "He's having something."

Hugh punches my arm and nearly makes me spill my drink. Fortunately he's a mate so I don't need to eat his head and spit it at Nora. I glower sourly and a look of something like recognition surfaces on his face. "You really don't know about this stuff, do you? Christ, Gabe! I'd have thought that after all the time you've spent at ours you'd have picked at least something up."

I shrug. I don't see knowledge of intimately beating people as a huge lacking. "Not like I have anyone to practice it with, and those clubs just aren't my scene."

Hugh takes a long drink, looking thoughtful. After a minute, it is very apparent that he's come to some sort of decision as he slams his pint down, takes my glass off me and drags me roughly to the bar by my coat. Suddenly, I've got the warm, leather-wrapped handle of a flogger in my fist, am being watched expectantly on all sides, and my intended victim has begun giggling nervously as all the blows have stopped.

The tails of the flogger hang limply, sheened with sweat and a faint splattering of beer. It's heavier than I would have thought, and I'd assumed it would be imbued with a violent sexual power that it would transfer to me to perform with. But it just hangs there, flaccid, and the seconds begin to drag out.

What the hell am I supposed to do with this? Perhaps I should rally against expectation and shove the hilt up this guy's arse, then invite the local children down to bat at the dangling flails like kittens at tassels. Or I could turn on the room, sadistic fetish gear on sadistic fetish gear: dodge the quirts and paddles they throw at me, duck the bit and ball gags they wield like maces. If I go down, nine inch metal points that stab from thigh high boots would be shoved down my mouth and out through my throat like demonic armoured penises. I could defeat them all then claim them as my filthy army and lay siege to the world, drowning cities in lubricant and rubbing ginger into the clits and penile glands of all who oppose me. It'd be a shiny PVC revolution: glorious, titillating and terrifying.

"Oh for fuck's sake, just hit him."

Hugh used his Dom voice and my arm is compelled to obey, slashing diagonally to lay the tails across the kid's shoulders with a loud slap. There's no rush of blood to my crotch but there is a definite buzz, an electrical thrill that runs through my brain-base. I can see why people like this. The little high abruptly evaporates when I feel a crack across my arse, the solid paddle striking hard enough to leave prickling heat spreading across my cheeks and thighs for several seconds. Hugh takes back the flogger, passes it to the original wielder and then meanders back to Nora. Nothing better occurs to me at this point but to follow.

"So there you go," Hugh concludes as I sit back down, emptying my glass this time before he can take it off me again. "What did you think?"

I elect not to answer that just yet as I need a bit of time to digest the giddy thrill of having held the position to inflict invited pain, and then the far more questionable and revealing emotional spasms resulting from being hit. I suspect I've roped myself into trying it again in the future to really clarify my thoughts on the matter. Very rudely, but sod it, I ask a question of my own in response to his. "So do you tend to do that drunk?"

"Me?" He seems affronted and I worry that I've committed some fetish faux-paus. "Hell no. I know some folks who do, but not us. Tonight's just a laugh. Safety, consent and sanity." Hugh stresses the last, ticking the triangle points off on his blunt fingers. "Some substance is alright if you can hold it, but I'd never do anything heavy whilst compromised."

Nora doesn't look proud. It's just a matter of fact.

The lights go out as another woman, dark and willowy, steps up to the bar. In the blackness, all we can see is the gentle flares of cigarette tips, bobbing lazily like fireflies, and the ethereal glow of the two stringy floggers in her hands. One is blue, the other green. She twirls and slashes them down in the same rolling, crossing motion that I've seen before in poi spinners, the glowing tails trailing smears of colour like the lit fire poi leave retinal stripes. The impacts are sharp and crackling. Pulling at the tape about his wrists, the guy keens a low, stuttered sound. We all watch in silence. After a minute, I wish she'd stop so I could get another drink.

* * *

The plane hits a pocket of cold air, plummets briefly, then climbs again without announcement. Tilley jerks awake from the turbulence and I stop glaring at the sudden, long streak from my pen long enough to offer her a peanut. She turns me down and pulls the thin but surprisingly soft blanket up to her chin, going back to sleep. I figure to try and pass out for the last few hours of the flight, too. Then I'll be back in England, seeking out the ungodly and the profane. It's going to be a good little holiday.

Chapter 4
—
To Market

"Bushes instead of fences, people walking their dogs down every street, fake columns on the houses. It's a disgrace of proper pretence given that a large proportion of the locals are FUCKING PERVERTS!"

I'm somewhat drunk and leaning out of the car window, screaming the last into the road. Tilley shrinks a little in the driver's seat, tugs oddly at her underwear and then sits up again. I throw myself back and light another cigarette.

"How fast are you going?" I demand, leaning across to try and see the speedometer on the wrong side of the car.

She shoves me back. "Same speed as you, so shut up." She goes back to ignoring me.

We'd booked into a little two star hotel in Cheltenham Spa. It's disgustingly pretty and snobbish. It's even got a Promenade for the sole purpose of strutting up and down the posh shops, admiring the uniform flower beds and the war monuments of the dead soldiers from God knows when and where. We picked Cheltenham because it was smack centre between all the really fetish-heavy spots, was a short drive from Bath, Ben's old stomping ground, and had The High Window hotel, which I demanded we stay at. I've been a fan of Raymond Chandler since staying in a house-swap villa in Florida with my family when I was thirteen and pulling a gritty detective book off the bookshelf. I've not looked at a woman or a gun the same way since.

Today we're driving to the Other Country Market, the big fetish bazaar held once a month in Twikham village. Through some research and expensive phone calls, we've discovered that the makers of the gimp hood that Ben died in are frequent stall owners at this market.

Tilley's driving because I couldn't face the twisting nightmare of the English motorway, and I'd opted to start getting drunk bright and early before we set off. She's not letting me drink in the rented car so we can get our deposit back, so I should be somewhere close to sober by the time we get there. I'm also chain smoking which always helps to sharpen out my mind.

We've dressed to blend in. I'm wearing all black, as is my understanding of heterosexual fetishists. All those chain-link vests and leather trousers scream "gay dominant priest looking for boyish men with tiny, permanently erect nipples," which I most certainly am not. Tilley has gone for the military look, wearing a red PVC jacket and micro-skirt belt thing that she bought off eBay. Inexplicably, she tore her fishnets before we got into the car, but she assures me that it was intentional. I told her to get her ridiculously tall platforms into the car and get driving.

Almost everyone in this country has a tiny car, I've observed. Hundreds of them, millions even, and they've actually crammed them full of apparently comfortable people. We overtake an old Mini hammering down the slow lane, engine screaming a suicidal-virgin song of pain and lust, the machine enjoying the speed in the same way that the occupants of the car are assured of their personal safety. Teenagers in there, all yuppies I'd wager, all leaking noise and hormones into a little tin car that'll just feed it back to them in an endless, reverberating fashion.

I wonder if it's possible to have an orgy in a Mini. The boot is more of a queer cupboard, so they could just keep lube and condoms in there, maybe a Taser and some waxing strips. I hear they keep a makeup artist on the set of porn films to cover pubic stubble, making the vagina, perineum and arsehole look more immaculate than they could ever actually be. Anal bleaching comes into it too somewhere, I'm sure. Apparently your arsehole has turned black by the time you get to sixty. I wonder how accurately mine tells of my age. I consider asking Tilley, but decide that that question is too obscene even for me. I settle for asking her if she thinks it's possible to have an orgy in the back of a Mini instead.

"Only if you take the front passenger seat out and cover the floor rails with something. Those things dig in like a bitch."

This answer satisfies me entirely and I go back to smoking in silence, watching the Mini shrinking in the rear view mirror until it's obscured by traffic and distance. I scratch at my crotch through the heavy dark denim. I decide that I should have brought more money. There's a horrible chance I might buy an old Mini now for the sake of 'research,' then butcher it into a nymphomaniac's driving paradise. I'd have mirrors and tiny cameras with screens stitched elegantly into the wipe-clean upholstered dashboard. A plunger of lubricant that was always full would be embedded into the side of the back wall, black and melding in perfectly with the interior so you could make a discreet push for more sauce if and when needed. Everything we got from the fair would be hung in tasteful, padded and buckled holsters from the ceiling, the tails from the floggers and whips held aloft in little pouches so as to be kept out of the way. The floor would be suede cushions filled with goose-down, the covers removable and machine washable. The windows would all be blacked out, and the rear ones would be mirrored as well. Black paint and chrome, leather seats, a mini-fridge tucked away stocked with water and champagne. Alternating cold water and warm tea whilst getting head feels fantastic, so I'd have to find space for a cup holder the right size to accommodate a Styrofoam cup most commonly found in take-away motorway rest stops. And mints. Mints feel tingly. There'd have to be a dedicated mint-box somewhere with a selection of strengths.

This intricate planning, doodling out diagrams and schematics in my journal, and working out how much it would cost to ship the final product back to the States occupies me wholly until we leave the motorway and plunge into the country roads that must have been designed by a three year old scribbling with crayons whilst having an epileptic fit. I can discern that we are in the country by the fact that we pass more pheasants, foxes and rabbits than people. By people, I mean a farmer on a combined harvester with its flashing amber light blown out. I advise Tilley that if we ram it, the Highway Code decrees that because of that light being out it would be his fault. Even in the bright light of midday, if that light goes out, then all twenty feet of farm equipment is rendered invisible and we could claim damages. Tilley throws a damp sponge at me. I didn't know that sponges were a necessary accessory in a car for wiping away the damp that collects on the windows and sunroof until we hit England. As I wipe off sponge-germs on the polyester seat covers, I decide that I could have happily continued with my life without knowing that.

Twikham, to my dismay, is barely a village. In fact, we drive right through it without noticing and have to creep back slowly to find its borders. It's not just hedges here but dry-walling, a reassuring layer of moss holding the chunky stones together about the equally mossy houses. No two buildings are alike, and aside from a tiny village hall, post office and a war monument, there's nothing here. Oh, but the cars are beginning to pile in, and there's nowhere to park within the glorified hamlet.

When we do finally stop on a grass verge, Tilley eyes my journal and then nods to the glove compartment. She's right. A hidden Dictaphone is much more suitable now. I also tuck away my phone, already aware of the no cameras policy of the place and knowing that no one is going to call me anyway. We get out of the car and I feel a sudden, strange pang that it isn't a Mini, and that we didn't have to weave and leaver ourselves out of the doors to avoid getting concussed. I ask Tilley if we can ask the rental company if they have any Minis we can use when we get back. She tells me to fucking sober up and to be quiet in the meantime.

Walking back up the side of the road beside sloping fields and curious cows, we find ourselves being passed by the rubber army in Fords and Rovers. Apparently the Other Country Market is the only real reason that people come here. Another tractor rumbles by and my too-sober head throbs with disappointment. Though a cunning name, I'd have hoped that the OCM would be for the elite of the villagers, bearing their pimped out harvesters and seeders, bouncing the tons of metal and plastic on their giant tires whilst LEDs cast out mangled electric blue lights from inside the cabins. There would be fairy lights about the prongs down to the baler, slasher or mower, which would be decorated with obscene gang-land phrases and cartoon sheep. Country girls in denim hot-pants and kerchief tops would wave the checker flags to start the drag races, caravan-pulls and steak roasting over the flame-equipped exhausts, and the meet would go on all night.

My schemes fizzle out when Tilley tells me that it wouldn't translate over the pond, thus there's no point in falling in love with the idea now. I take us into the tiny shop to console myself with chocolate, briefly fondling the fresh eggs laid out in the chicken-shaped basket just inside the door. The woman behind the counter scowls at my touching, folding her arms across the great wet sandbags of her breasts. I meekly take up an egg and buy it for far too much money, throwing in a Twix and a packet of cigarettes as well. Tilley appears with stale cookies and I take out my wallet again. The cashier doesn't pay any heed to her attire. Apparently the locals are quite used to the weird folk descending upon them en masse once a month.

Replenished, and with my egg hidden underneath a hedge as a donation to any passing fox or badger, we make our way to the town hall. Outside looks innocuous enough, with a village notice board advertising the next meeting of the wine tasting club; the winner of the raffle (Michael Hulmes – prize: one giant teddy); and an advertisement for a used two-storey deluxe hamster cage. I am informed that I am not allowed a hamster and sulk suitably.

Heading around the building, we see that the market is half open-air as it spills out of the back doors, bearing its black and shiny offerings to the sun. The tarpaulins are tied and weighted down with concrete bricks which the pony girls and training-collar wearing submissives step over primly. We're directed by one woman holding a leash that splits off to claim two nubile young things around to the front of the hall again to pay our admission.

Chapter 5

The Hood

As we get close to the entrance, I feel the apparition of a chain leading from Tilley's hand to my neck materialising. Though this is my money, my trip and largely my investigative case, she's the one in charge here, standing four clean inches taller than me in her absurd boots and stomping off in the lead. This might work to my favour though, so I follow along quietly and pay my entry fee when we get inside.

Before we get to the actual area where the indoor stalls are set up, there's a table freshly leafleted with all sorts of services that an aspiring and veteran fetishist might want. I'm delighted to see that there is a handyman advertising to install electrics, heating and plumbing into dungeons and specially-equipped play areas, saving the potential embarrassment of finding the plumber masturbating over your new stocks when you come back with his coffee. Picking up a few of the flyers, I weigh up the pros and cons of Tilley having her labia pumped full of saline by a Domme nurse. It'd be hilarious, certainly, but I know my mind, and I know that the humour of it would wear off far quicker than the saline would, and I'd just end up sulking because the woman I'm with looks to have bigger balls than me. I put the leaflet back down and catch up to Tilley, checking her crotch just to reassure myself that it's stayed petite and minimally fleshy in my absence.

The stall owners all look normal and friendly, their specialist wares laid out professionally. A lot of it's handmade, and we spend some time testing the weight of spreader bars and thigh cuffs. There's a cuff for everything now, and I see a black arm straitjacket that laces up the forearms into a straight, posture-perfect line. Leather harnesses are also sold in this heady smelling corner, and I watch a young woman getting sized up into her own custom one. The owner keeps swapping around lengths of leather and metal poppers, accommodating her plump thighs and thin waist. Very hourglass, and unlike the fashion industry, this man is working to fit and compliment her shape perfectly. There's a small crowd watching him work, admiring his skill and craftsmanship. She's fully dressed and smiling. It's a good atmosphere.

At the next stall Tilley has me buy her a collar, telling me that if it looks like we're genuinely here to buy stuff, then people will be more willing to talk to us. We haven't seen a stall that sells hoods yet, but it might be outside near the demonstration area. Apparently there's something with bullwhips scheduled for three and all we have to do is wander out and watch. We can even take beer.

Two hours pass without my notice and we haven't even begun to start questioning yet. Tilley is having too much fun playing with everything and swiping my credit card, and I'm having too much fun watching. She has me lash her gently with a purple suede and leather flogger whilst the stall owner instructs me on my whipping style. Rolling wrists and a crossing motion are the key, apparently. Keeping it all fluid and smooth, keeping the strength constant, are things I gain some skill in quickly, and I buy the thing just as a testament to that. Tilley is delighted and asks if she can keep it when we get back home. Bitch.

By the doors leading outside things get really

frightening. There's a stall dedicated to electric toys that hums and buzzes continuously. I refuse to have my arm touched by a Magic Wand and Tilley doesn't make a point to go over to the woman offering either. More disconcerting buzzing comes from a stall with no apparent source of sound. That is, until we see the neat little glasses lined up. It's an engraving machine. We could get a little whip or a slave boy on a glass if we wanted to. "Isn't that nice?" Tilley coos. I'm busy gawping at the nearby embroidery hand towels that read in such mix and match pairs as: Master and Slave; Mistress and Girl or Boy; and Daddy and Precious. I immediately buy a Master and Mistress set, ignoring the seller's frown at my choice but thoroughly pleased with myself for the purchase.

Finally we get to the stall we're looking for: the makers and sellers of Ben's hood. It's outside, near the fence, where a willow tree is trying to join in. Tilley stands close to me and picks through the hoods and blindfolds, feeling their sturdy linings and detachable mouthpieces. Everything is leather or latex, sturdy and durable. You can get accessories that will force a mouth open in a perfect O, will inflate to playfully threaten to asphyxiate them, or will shove a rubber dick down their throat so you don't have to. She's surreptitiously listening to everything I'm saying to the leather-clad man behind the racks, and the seller seems perfectly amicable and happy to answer all my questions, utterly unaware of the Dictaphone recording everything in my breast pocket.

I learnt about as much as I could have from the Internet about hoods, but there's a personal and genuinely passionate current running through the information he's giving me that really hits something. There's a genuine affection and interest as well as an assured knowledge of his wares. The hoods objectify gimps and mask identity, making them as much an object as a strap-on or a paddle in a scene. This is usually mutually desired, or at least desired on one side and exploited on the other. It provides almost complete sensory deprivation, meaning that all focus is on sensation: pain and pleasure. I've played with this concept before with blindfolds, and I am tempted by the mindfuck of a hood at this point. It also renders the wearer silent, which I can imagine more than one previous partner of mine seeing as a godsend.

The seller hands me a leather hood to demonstrate his points, turning it over in my hands to show me the opening at the back that extends to a hole for the neck, sealed closed with a cord. The latex ones stretch enough not to warrant such a fastener. I immediately prefer the leather ones, and from the warmth of it in my hands, I know I'll be walking away with this piece. There's a good chance that I'll never have the balls to wear it, or see anyone in it, but it'll be a testament to today, and to this kinked road that Ben's buried body is leading us down.

There are no eyeholes in this particular model, though I am welcome to swap it for one that has zips over the eyes. I prefer it with the extra step away from an executioner's mask. There are nostril openings and a small mouth hole that can be plugged with gags that strap over the smooth, shining body of the hood. He shows me a funnel and tube gag, only offering it to my hands rather than forcing me to hold it. I can pour any liquid I want down it, and they'd have to swallow. He doesn't look at Tilley, only me. No assumptions. Whether I'm to be wearing it or her, it doesn't bother him at all. Hell, I think he'd let us both try it on if we wanted.

I'm told the benefit of the leather hood is that it renders the wearer totally blind, and that if I wanted full deprivation in a spandex hood I'd need to purchase a blindfold as well. He'd do me a discount though, since it was my first time and I seemed so keen to own. Another option was Darlex, which wasn't as porous, but he didn't have any of those on him. He'd bring one to the market next month for me, or take my address and send it to me within the week. Peripherally, I saw Tilley smiling, and I suddenly wanted to buy this guy a beer and a Mars bar. He was just so damn nice. I didn't care if this thing was forty five pounds. I was going to buy it, just off of his charm.

Finally, I ask the million-dollar question: could a hood kill a person? "Definitely," is the immediate, firm and sombre reply. Potentially, hoods and gags are extremely dangerous due to the ease with which all access to air can be blocked, resulting in rapid and the total, non-fun kind of asphyxiation. It's wise to use a hood with a mouth hole and a gag over the hood that can be taken off quickly. Failing that, the surgical scissors that are an essential item in all kits can be used to cut through the strap. There's something else beneath his level knowingness. I wonder if news of Ben's death has come to him with the label that it was his hood that was involved. I think it might have.

I don't ask him if he remembers Ben from whenever Ben stood by this stall and bought a hood, probably similar to the one I'm holding right now. If he had bought a hood at all, that is. The partner could have. He hasn't asked me my name, and doubtless that's a sort of policy—don't ask unless offered or necessary. The real answer I needed is whether or not these things can kill, accidentally and thus intentionally, and the answer is yes. I pay out the money and try to leave him a tip, but he refuses and claps me on the shoulder as he hands the weighty black bag to me. I look to see if Tilley has picked up anything she wants, but she hasn't and her smile has slipped into something limply lukewarm. I gently take her wrist, thank the seller again and lead her towards the other side of the market. A bullwhipping demonstration might be just the thing to ease us out of this quiet little rut we've slipped into.

Chapter 6

—

Nuggets

Three days later we're still in England and planning our next angle of attack. Through some snooping around, we have discovered that Ben visited a professional dominatrix once, just once, back in his closeted "I'm only kinky" days. Tilley and I currently sit in a McDonalds working out our cover stories. With neither of us really being inherent fetishists, we're going to need to get into character when we visit the innocuous building that houses a reception, a dungeon and mock hospital room.

I printed some questionnaires off the Internet in a cyber café earlier this morning, and now, as Tilley returns to our plastic table and bolted down swivel chairs by the window, I arrange them out of the way so she can set down our chicken nugget Happy Meals. She doesn't take much interest in her questionnaire, its purpose being for us to determine what kind of fetishists we want to appear as to the senior Mistress. Instead, she unwraps her anthropomorphised toy cat, takes mine and then makes them have clacky, plastic intercourse on the table. Using a floppy chip as a rudimentary whip, Puss One starts flaying Puss Two, who is wailing in a hissing—yet delighted—fashion.

The parents at the next table watch with wide eyes until I click my stare to theirs, and then they go back to forcing their kids to colour in the picture drawn on too-shiny paper with too-waxy crayons. I take a ball-point pen out of my jacket pocket and regard the first page of the surprisingly long and thorough questionnaire.

It's designed for Submissives to be provided to their Dominants or "Tops" before sceneing with them, providing a quick overview of limits, favourites and a means of finding common ground to play or negotiate over. As we're visiting a Dominatrix under the guise of wanting to be abused in some form, this seems fitting. Each item needs to have a Yes or No put next to it first to indicate if I have ever done that particular activity, or rather had it done to me. Next, I say how I feel about it by rating it as a No or on a scale of nought to five, nought indicating that I wouldn't ordinarily do it but I would be willing to if it would please the Dominant. One through five indicate varying stages of enjoyment and willingness, with five being a "wild for it" number. No is a hard limit and wouldn't be done under any circumstances.

There's even more detail to go into that I'll skip, such as whether I'd only do some activities with a current sex or play partner, or partners, and those that I'd be happier doing with casual play-partners. It takes me about twenty minutes of alternating between writing, thinking and eating my Happy Meal to complete the profile of my fictional fetishist self. I'm quite pleased with the end result and make a note to stick it in my journal for my personal amusement on long flights. There's nothing like reading this sort of thing directly in the eye line of the stranger seated next to you, who somehow disappears during the flight and walks away from you on the verge of a jog when you find each other again in the arrivals terminal.

Submissive BDSM Play Partner Check List

	Experience	**Willingness**
Abrasion	No	No
Age play	Yes	2
Anal	No	0
Anal plugs (small)	Yes	5
Anal plugs (large)	Yes	4
Anal plugs (amusingly shaped)	Yes	5
Anal plug (public, under clothes)	Yes	3
Animal roles	No	2
Arm & leg sleeves (armbinders)	No	0
Asphyxiation	No	No
Auctioned for charity	No	No
Bathroom use control	No	No
Bestiality	No	0
Beating (soft)	Yes	5
Beating (hard)	Yes	4
Blindfolds	Yes	5
Being serviced (sexual)	Yes	5
Being bitten	Yes	3
Breast/chest bondage	No	0
Breath control	No	No
Branding	No	0
Boot worship	No	2
Bondage (light)	Yes	5
Bondage (heavy)	Yes	2
Bondage (multi-day)	Yes	2
Bondage (public, under clothing)	Yes	2
Breast/chest whipping	No	0
Brown showers (scat)	No	0

Bukkake	No	0
Cages (locked inside of)	Yes	4
Catheterization	Yes	No
Caning	Yes	3
Cells/Closets (locked inside of)	Yes	4
Chastity belts	Yes	3
Chauffeuring	Yes	0
Choking	No	No
Clothespins	Yes	No
Cock worship	No	No
Collars (worn in private)	No	0
Collars (worn in public)	No	No
Competitions (with other Subs)	No	No
Corsets (wearing)	No	0
Cuffs (leather)	Yes	5
Cuffs (metal)	Yes	5
Cutting	Yes	0
Cutting (decorative, scarification)	No	1
Dilation	N/A	-
Double penetration	Yes	1
Electricity	No	2
Email sex	Yes	3
Enemas	Yes	4
Enforced chastity	No	2
Examinations (physical)	Yes	3
Exercise (forced/required)	No	No
Exhibitionism (friends)	No	No
Exhibitionism (strangers)	Yes	No
Eye contact restrictions	No	No
Face slapping	Yes	4
Fantasy abandonment	No	1
Fantasy rape	Yes	1
Fantasy gang-rape	Yes	1
Fisting (anal)	Yes	3

Fisting (vaginal)	N/A	-
Following orders	Yes	5
Foot worship	Yes	5
Forced dressing	No	1
Forced homosexuality	Yes	1
Forced masturbation	Yes	3
Forced nudity (private)	Yes	3
Forced nudity (around others)	Yes	1
Forced servitude	Yes	2
Full head hoods	No	No
Gags (cloth)	No	1
Gags (rubber)	No	1
Gags (tape)	Yes	3
Gates of Hell (male)	No	No
Genital sex	Yes	5
Genital torture (stem ginger, etc)	No	No
Given away to another Dom (temp)	No	No
Given away to another Dom (perm)	No	No
Golden showers	Yes	1
Hairbrush spankings	No	2
Hair pulling	No	3
Hand jobs (giving)	No	3
Hand jobs (receiving)	Yes	5
Harems (serving w/other subs)	No	1
Harnessing (leather)	No	2
Harnessing (rope)	Yes	2
Having food chosen for you	No	1
Having clothing chosen for you	No	1
Head (giving fellatio)	No	1
Head (receiving fellatio)	Yes	5
High heel worship	Yes	4
Homage with tongue (non-sexual)	Yes	2
Hot oils (on genitals)	Yes	No
Hot oils (on body)	Yes	2

Hot waxing	No	No
Housework (doing)	No	1
Human puppy dog	No	No
Humiliation (private)	Yes	1
Humiliation (public)	Yes	No
Hypnotism	No	2
Ice cubes	Yes	2
Infantilism	No	No
Initiation rites	No	1
Injections	No	1
Intricate (Japanese) rope bondage	No	2
Interrogations	Yes	1
Kidnapping	No	1
Kneeling	Yes	3
Leather clothing	Yes	5
Leather restraints	Yes	5
Lectures for misbehaviour	No	4
Licking (non-sexual)	No	3
'Magick'	No	No
Manacles & Irons	Yes	5
Manicures (giving)	Yes	4
Massage (giving)	No	4
Massage (receiving)	No	4
Medical scenes	No	3
Modelling for erotic photos	No	No
Mouth bits	No	2
Mummification	No	1
Nipple clamps	Yes	3
Nipple weights	Yes	2
Oral/anal play (rimming)	Yes	3
Over-the-knee spanking	Yes	3
Orgasm denial	Yes	1
Orgasm control	No	1
Outdoor scenes	No	1

Outdoor sex	Yes	3
Phone sex (serving Dom)	No	4
Phone sex (serving Dom's friends)	No	4
Piercing (temporary, play-pierce)	No	2
Piercing (permanent)	No	2
Prison scenes	No	3
Pony slave	No	1
Public exposure	No	No
Pussy/cock whipping	Yes	2
Pussy worship	Yes	4
Riding crops	Yes	2
Riding the "horse" (crotch tort.)	No	No
Rituals	No	1
Religious scenes	No	1
Restrictive rules on behaviour	No	1
Rubber/latex clothing	No	1
Rope body harness	No	2
Saran wrapping	Yes	4
Scratching - getting	Yes	4
Scratching - giving	No	4
Sensory deprivation	No	2
Serving	No	2
Serving as art	No	1
Serving as ashtray	Yes	1
Serving as furniture	Yes	1
Serving as a maid	No	1
Serving as toilet	No	No
Serving as waitress/waiter	Yes	3
Serving orally (sexual)	No	3
Serving other doms (supervised)	No	1
Serving other doms (unsupervised)	No	1
Sexual deprivation (short term)	No	No
Sexual deprivation (long term)	No	No
Shaving (body hair)	Yes	1

Shaving (head hair)	Yes	No
Sleep deprivation	Yes	1
Sleepsacks	No	1
Slutty clothing (private)	Yes	1
Slutty clothing (public)	No	No
Spanking	Yes	4
Spandex clothing	No	2
Speech restrictions (when, what)	No	No
Speculums (Anal)	Yes	3
Speculums (vaginal)	N/A	-
Spreader bars	Yes	5
Standing in corner	No	3
Stocks	No	4
Strait jackets	No	3
Strap-on-dildos (sucking on)	Yes	4
Strap-on-dildos (penetrated by)	Yes	3
Strap-on-dildos (wearing)	No	2
Strapping (full body beating)	No	2
Suspension (upright)	No	2
Suspension (inverted)	No	1
Suspension (horizontal)	No	3
Supplying new partners for Dom	No	No
Swallowing semen	Yes	No
Swallowing urine	Yes	No
Swapping (with one other couple)	No	1
Swinging (multiple couples)	No	1
Tattooing	No	No
Teasing	Yes	3
Tickling	No	2
Torture scenes	Yes	2
Triple penetration	No	No/?
Uniforms	Yes	5
Including others	No	2
Vaginal dildo	N/A	-

Verbal humiliation	Yes	2
Vibrator on genitals	Yes	4
Voyeurism (watching others)	No	4
Voyeurism (your Dom w/others)	No	4
Video (watching others)	Yes	5
Video (recordings of you)	No	No
Water torture	No	No
Wearing symbolic jewellery	No	No
Whipping	Yes	4
Wooden paddles	Yes	3
Wrestling	No	4

Good God, you can have a lot done to you. Looking back over the list makes me feel vaguely giddy. Though I know a lot of people within the fetish scene, I had no idea it was so expansive and clique-ridden: the spitroasters and the suspension bondage specialists; the strap-on Nazis and the nipple-clamp nuts; and then the jacks of all trades. I aimed my character to be primarily obsessed with having things put in his rectum, and though I knew I should pick up the hood and asphyxiation just for the journalistic sake of understanding what it was we are investigating, I can't bring myself to. Part of me already knows that the hood laid out on the pillow of the hotel to alarm the cleaner will end up sold on eBay or given as a gift to Hugh and Nora, but I might just keep it as a trophy.

I look out the window to remind myself of the world outside the scene. A woman walks her fat yellow Labrador past, the dog walking like a trolley with two wonky wheels. Its flesh jiggles back and forth around its barrel torso, and I watch the hypnotic movement until they clear the window. The kid's meal, surprisingly, hasn't filled a hole the size of a gnat's cock. I'll be pillaging the menu again, then.

Sliding the crayons over my complimentary colouring picture whilst Tilley finally starts filling in her questionnaire, I note that she puts 'No' on asphyxiation too. However, she does put a '2' in willingness to wear a hood, so I might just get some use out of the thing yet. For research purposes, of course.

Chapter 7

Wet Reflections

Later, I'm sprawled across the hotel bed feeling sick and bloated, coming down from sugar and salt. I've squirmed and fidgeted, turned the wafer pillow into a sodding origami sculpture, and I've come to the conclusion that I cannot deal with my body in this state whilst conscious anymore. I demand a substance from Tilley, any kind: something that will claw about my mouth, have sex with my tongue, spit down my throat and finally knock me out. She says that she could fetch me a hooker who'll do pretty much just that. I tell her to go die in a fire, but to throw me my prescription sleeping pills first.

The pills are fantastically strong. Within minutes of taking them in the past, I have hallucinated wildly about keyboards strangling my head with cold, black thighs and then slept dreamlessly for nine hours. The last time I took them, I lay staring down the opening of a brown paper bag on my chest and at the blond puppy peering out at me. I'd much prefer such imagery over this Happy Meal induced sugar-coma. Tilley remains unaffected, and happily tells me that she left the pills behind because she didn't think they'd make it through customs. I demand alcohol. She tells me to get it myself. I get up, puke, then make my way to the door, grabbing the essentials for short-term survival on the way out. These are largely in the form of filter-tips and sunglasses even though it's completely overcast.

The world is grey outside, bleak and dreary. The

trees look sallow and washed down, colour leaking into the tarmac and pavements where it is drowned by yet more grey and blackness, for a touch of variety. I stumble to the corner-shop that has turned into my cigarette refuge, and demand a bottle of scotch from the Indian man behind the bar. I follow him round to the area blocked off from me by a wall of boxes, stacked plastic crates and general crap. He points at bottles. I squint and wave indiscriminately, unable to see that far when my body feels like a zeppelin that has crashed onto the residents of the Burning Man festival, who continue to party strangely, and unwanted, beneath my engorged flesh. I hand him a purple note, pocket the shrapnel and tear into the neck of the bottle the moment I get outside.

After a few long swallows, I gain some clarity and realise that I can't go back to that hotel again just now. I need air that isn't shared with fetishists, drug addicts and Tilley. I take myself down the road to the park, feeling my clothes moisten in the almost imperceptible drizzle that decides to accompany me.

I find a bench and sit, then inexplicably I begin to think about Laura. It's pathetic, sitting here with a cigarette in one hand and a big bottle of whiskey in the other, on a park bench, in the rain, thinking about an old relationship, but fuck it – this week's been weird enough already. Some cliché can do a man good. I let this sink in as I watch a droplet coalesce on my lax fingertip, quivering with its bulk before peeling free and shattering on the concrete next to the bench leg.

In the closing years of my parent's lives, we used to move around a lot. Not just towns, but countries. Laura moved around with us too sometimes, and one day we found ourselves leaving a newly rented house in waist deep brown water, the county flooded out of homes and sense. Laura and I waded out together to the city centre to see everything happen. This was all far before I gained an aversion to physical contact, so I held her wrist, alternating with her hand, as I dragged her slighter weight through the torrents. Where the burst river was close we had to grasp at the cars and lampposts to stay upright. The water had soaked up to our chests, and it stank. We were doing our best not to think of what was in it, particularly when our boots compressed something soft and rubbery that slid out the sides and whipped away with the tide.

We fumbled out a bench and stood on it to take a break from the cloying water that resisted us. After a few minutes, we had the bemusing chance to see a car peeling through the water, hit another submerged car in a deep dip and come to an abrupt stop. The windows wouldn't open and the water was rising fast in the car. The driver had to haul himself out through the sun roof. I saw five unlit cigarettes splayed out of his lips, his neck straining up to keep them dry as the empty box bobbed around the passenger headrest. Laura and I went and sat on his roof after he left, feeling cold and hungry but incredibly aware. Neither of us had ever seen anything like it.

We spent hours there. Kids up to their handlebars forced their bikes through, their pristine white trainers linked by laces and hanging from their necks as they peddled past. A dinghy cruised by, asked if we were stranded and needed help, and then carried on into town after we told them we were just watching for now. A man was systematically sweeping the edges of the new river with a big net. We asked him why, and he said he was catching the escaped Koi

Carp. Whether or not any of them were his to begin with, he didn't say, but there was an evil sort of brilliance in his plan. I wondered if anyone would resort to battering and frying the fish when the panic-buyers stripped the shops and attacked the incoming trucks, wrestling water and bread from the torn-tarpaulin backs.

We knocked on doors and made sure people were alright on the way back. The water inside the hallways was no different to that out in the street, and though some were grey with shock, others were just wading through it without a glance. Just getting on with it. The bed and breakfast places were full, taking in stranded drivers when the dark was creeping in and filling them with coffee and tea. The water was still on for the time being back home, so I took Laura upstairs and washed us both down in the shower. The plant would have to be turned off soon and cleaned out for some time after, so I was thorough. She shaved her legs and I conditioned my hair for once. We filled ourselves with the smell of coconut and vanilla, got the smell of the wet streets off of us. The next day we went trekking off to find and buy a camping stove because the power looked to be going the same way.

This was all the last real adventure we had together before the end. She left me before I found my parents dead. It had been coming for some weeks, but maybe if I hadn't turned so unhinged after the funeral we could have made another go of it. I got very wasted one morning and decided that that was exactly the thing to do. A few weeks later I had my third restraining order against me and no Laura. So, that was all a bit shit, really. I've always had a problem with turning a situation that's tense but bearable into a night in a police station and a fine.

Fucked off with this train of thought now, I take a long, furious suck from a fresh cigarette followed by an even longer drink from the bottle. A quarter is gone now and the mist has let up, so it's safe to take out the BDSM sheet and review just what I've set myself up for. It's stayed dry in my jacket, and the crispness of it surprises my fingertips which had grown used to rubbing warm, moist wood. Scanning through, I notice with some surprise the lack of animals in it. Not that I'd touch it with a bridge support beam, but it'd be nice to have the choice, particularly with the more imaginative practises outside of straightforward bestiality. Just to have the pleasure of being able to turn them down.

I've indirectly encountered gerbilling through the medical community. Stories about gerbils, mice and hamsters being recovered, limp and sodden, from deep inside someone's anus. Shining a light up through a clear speculum and seeing a nose and blank, bulbous black eyes staring back. Must be a shock. Apparently it's the death throes that are the thrill—claw and tooth scrabbling and mashing around the rubbery, crinkled rectal walls, squeaks muffled by lube and mucus until it ultimately dies huddled against the quivering prostate. Users can only hope the furry sex-plugs come back out again on their own, rather than have a very awkward and damning visit to the doctors. Apparently, the real danger is when they escape out of the condom, if that's your like, and don't asphyxiate. I've heard stories of hamsters staying there for days, with the contemplated methods of removal ranging from eating a curry and gassing the thing out to shoving a cat up there, though the latter risks simply leaving the subject with a larger mammal up their arse.

My head lolls back and I spend an unknown amount of time staring into space, the beat of the conga suddenly and inexplicably drifting into my brain. In my mind's eye, I can see a chain of hamsters, tied to one another like spelunkers with strawberry liquorice laces, exploring a cramped cave, the leader gripping a tiny torch between his curved yellow jaws. After a few minutes of astonishment that my brain can produce this image of conga-dancing, spelunking arse hamsters, I take a self-medicating dose of whiskey and block it out. It's clearly time to go back to the hotel.

Chapter 8

Whiplash

Tilley's on the phone when I get back, and I can only hope she's not doing some freelance sex-line talk. Dial in, insert code, accept calls, accept verbal insults, receive money. Her voice box can be a whore, greased up for smooth rumbles, titillating purrs and false orgasmic moans. She occasionally works as one of the freelances from the main call-in companies and takes "those" calls. What's worse is I've seen her yawn through them, painting her toenails with one hand whilst she slaps cheap bacon against her shoulder by the phone receiver, occasionally dripping yogurt onto herself. Some cheesy sitcom is usually on with the volume turned down and she has to muffle out giggles. However, this doesn't seem to be one of those calls, so I take my hand off my crotch and sit down, rolling the whiskey under the bed where I hear it clunk against a wooden support. Tilley extends a long, bare leg and waves her toes at me.

I ask who it was just before she hangs up; overlapping an insight into this room into the ending segment of the conversation she'd been having with X. She tosses a pack of cigarettes into my lap, meaning that that this could be stupendously wonderful, like a religious leader going nuts and hanging paedophiles by their necks and scrotums in an all-night killing spree that spans parishes, or stupendously horrific like swimming into a warm patch in a freezing cold pool, feeling momentary relief before the urea reality sinks in, with perhaps something relating to kittens and toasters on top for that extra painful zing.

"I've got us in at the dominatrix house, and then I've done one better," she announces, bringing her legs crossed up onto the bed and working her fingers through her toes.

"Gotten us a meeting with the senior whip-bearer? Are you going to make me dress up somehow for that?" It seems like the sort of thing she'd do to me. I stayed over her place a few months ago and heard something moving in the middle of the night. I pummelled it with a nine iron, only to discover that it was the pet she hadn't told me she'd gotten. She's hasn't gotten me back for that yet.

She beams as I light up, either ignoring my second question or beginning to plan something now that I've psychically given her the idea. "Actually, I tracked down the woman that Ben scened with: Mistress Ram."

Impressive. "How did you manage that in the short time that I spent anesthetising myself?"

"You've been gone four hours." I nod, smoke, gesture for her to continue. "I told them that I had a friend who'd had the most amazing time with her a few years ago, and since they take everyone's details, they could tell me who did it. Ram used to work in the house but went solo a few years ago. I've got her number and address." She twists about so I can see the details scrawled in biro across her thigh. "How far away is Surrey?"

"For a witness as powerful as Ram, pretty damn close."

* * *

Against my better judgement, we have not set up

camp in the woods but acquired another hotel room. It took the better part of the afternoon to get here, our rented car laden with sherbet flying saucers, limp sandwiches and litres upon litres of Coke that had to be shipped into the room. Tilley has advised that I not be off my face when I meet Ram, as this will likely result in my swift disposal from her home and mind. And that wouldn't help Ben at all.

The cottage is not what I had expected from an experienced, formerly senior, Mistress. I'm told the dungeon is downstairs when Tilley runs a hand over the hefty oak door, padlocked shut 'for when the grandkids are over.' They don't know what she does. She keeps her working life separate and they all think she does something with computers from home. Helpfully, her computer array does look vast and impressive, backlit with blue lights and surrounded by tall, curved speakers. Clearly, caning people works for a living.

Mistress Ram is stately in presence, even when wearing soft brown trousers and a woollen top. Our first contact was by phone, and as I explained that I had never been worked over by a professional before, she offered to have me come around so we could talk in person to arrange my scene. Tilley told me that this didn't usually seem to be the case, but that I sounded pathetic. We'd brought our checklists, filled in and committed to memory, as she would find this information helpful.

Ram sits us both on the sofa and takes a place on a taller chair on the other side of the low coffee table. Sitting higher than us, though the setting and situation are relaxed, she is still potently in charge. We give her our sheets and she scans through them approvingly. "So, what did you two have in mind? Is there a specific scene that you would like to have?"

We'd planned all this out this morning. I had told Tilley what we were going to say and do, and Tilley had nodded and smoked petulantly at being told. I leant forward to speak, but found Tilley's hand on my knee and her voice slicing in, abruptly cutting me off before I could draw the breath for words.

"Well, Mistress, I fantasise about being left on a medical bed, with something holding me in suspense. Like, clamps or a freezing plug. And then I'd love to hear you doing something to him where I couldn't see you. Something long and enduring, violent and preferably anally-related. I'd like to lie there on that bed and think about you penetrating him with implements. Cold ones."

I don't understand what's happening. Tilley has the audacity not to even look at me during that little speech, smiling benignly and giving a fake squirm of pleasure and anticipation. To my horror, Ram smiles approvingly, inviting Tilley further along this violent deviation from the plan which will undoubtedly lead to awful acts being perpetrated upon my suddenly rubbery and unstable anus.

"He'll resist you, because he likes the fight, but he'll do as he's told. Won't you?" She grins at me, her eyes narrowed fractionally in that way that tells me in no uncertain terms that I'm in it deep here.

Unable to speak I just nod. Male submissives are the most common out of all the fetish subgroups anyway, with female submissives being the least. Ram is taking Tilley and me as a couple. I'm Tilley's bitch. I have a compelling urge to immediately smoke myself to death.

Mistress Ram shifts back and crosses her legs, arranging her hands across her raised knee. She looks straight at me. "So, from your sheet and what your Domme tells me, you wish to serve me, be restrained and then penetrated noisily so your Domme can hear you for her own pleasure. Is that correct?"

I nod stiffly, the only way I'm going to be stiff for a very long time after this. Though this is fulfilling a certain masochistic curiosity, it's also scaring all sorts of stuff out of me. "Yes, and my subsequent erection would blot out China."

Ram grins and looks to Tilley. "Are his erections to be punished?"

Tilley doesn't look at me, though I get the feeling she wants to. As the submissive, I don't have any right to expect such attention. Apparently.

"Absolutely. Every time. Kick it away if you have to. He really likes that."

I hate her.

* * *

My instinctive response to all of this was to find a large supermarket on the way home: one the size that accommodates stupid family spin-off aisles in addition to food and toilet paper. I purchase three two-litre bottles of mineral water, four tubes of KY jelly and the largest water pistol they stocked. This was my gut reaction to what Tilley had set me up for. The sales assistant gave me an odd look at the cash register, and Tilley did nothing in helping the situation by dumping a can of whipped cream and a pepper on the conveyer belt. I wasn't aware she had picked those up. I didn't want to think about why. The worst part about all this is the fact we don't have sex.

Back at the hotel, I resist the urge to thrust Tilley's head under the hot faucet and take a seat on the bed, squeezing the KY jelly into the unscrewed hole in the tank of the water pistol. Tilley dumps herself in the uncomfortable wooden chair on the opposite side of the room, clearly wary to be sitting beside me. This pleases me, and I squeeze the lubricant tube with extra vigour.

"You know you had this coming," she announces suddenly, slipping off her shoes and bringing her heels to tuck at her thighs, reaching around and wrapping her hands around the arches of her feet. The under soles are pale and crinkled. Her posture is defensive.

"I know, and it's fine. Gotta lay myself down like Jesus in the pursuit of truth, haven't I? I'd expected that from the start. I'll just block it out. Make the necessary noises and then limp out like John Wayne after thrusting a cactus up his arse." I pick up the second tube and commence squeezing violently. "What was up with all that hearing me but not seeing me shit? I don't remember that being on your sheet."

Tilley's smile spreads like oil through water, and she tips her head back at the apparent brilliance of it. "If she's busy with you, I can go look at her computer. She wasn't going to tell us about Ben. Pro-Dommes don't work like that. There's a code or something. But, because she's a professional, everything will be on her computer. All his turn-ons, his turn-offs. Everything. If breath control or something we can link to the gimp hood is in there, we can know for sure if he was into that stuff."

We fall into silence, albeit comfortable, and I've begun pouring the first bottle of water into the oily hole when she speaks again. "You know, I still don't buy the whole way we're going about this. I still think we should have gone straight to Carl. If we'd have just questioned him, figured out if he was there or not, we could have worked out between us if he was lying."

I screw the cap back onto the tank and take the pistol by the barrel and handle, shaking it firmly and erratically a dozen times to get the lubricant and water mixed up fully. To Tilley, I'm sure this seems a pointless exercise. To me, however, it's coping and preparing. "That would have been obvious, and obvious accomplishes nothing." I hold out the pistol at an awkward angle, my arm shaking. "And besides, where's the adventure in going straight to Carl?"

She tips sideways in the chair, teetering on the edge. "I see your point." She takes the water pistol. "What exactly am I supposed to do with this?"

Midway through her asking I'm on my feet, beginning to strip. "Use your God-given imagination and just keep spraying."

Chapter 9

Darth Bitch

I'm trying not to think about this too much. My arse cheeks are sweating and the hole is scrunching up like some badly knotted ball of elastic bands, misshapen and taut. My hands are tied though I can still feel my fingers, white as they are, as they clutch the edges of the vaulting horse that I'm so openly splayed across. Mistress Ram's got my ankles down as well, my legs spread wide and tilting my body down. The equipment is some horrific amalgamation of a laboratory table and children's gym equipment. In fact, I think I've seen this exact horse that I'm naked and shivering on in the children's section of IKEA. Those damn Swedes. What unholy inbreeding of furniture is this?

Ram is talking almost continuously about each and every instrument of buggery she's going to shove up my unsteady anal passage. I'm making all the appropriate grovellings and pleadings, being good and loud to fulfil the sick requirements of the scene Tilley promised. It'll give her some cover and make this whole ordeal sound far worse than it actually is, so I can shove the lube gun up her arse later as revenge.

Lubricant is diving inside there now, cold and peculiar. It sort of bubbles wetly on the way back out, making your cheeks squirm and tighten against each other, like a guinea pig with chronic diarrhoea, trying desperately not to shit-spray where it eats, fearing it would drown amidst stained and floating wood chippings in its precious little home. When the plastic box base reached full capacity, the bitty sludge would seep through the wire bars, amassing in chewy clogs at the edges. The guinea pig, trying desperately not to be dragged down by the weight of its own excrement saturated fur, would press against the bars and unsteadily begin to climb, making a desperate bid for air and freedom. But the bars would be too slippery, and it'd fall and tumble back with no hope of resurfacing from the soft brown pool that swiftly takes residence up its nose, in addition to everywhere else. I force away thoughts of furry twitching cheeks and velvety pink noses as Ram finally takes up the first implement.

I've talked to homosexuals about this stuff before—namely the *how does stuff go up if it's designed to have stuff come down* aspect. "Push out" was always the surprising and unrequested advice. I close my eyes, my voice falling into the recording of pleasure I've mentally pre-set for it. I picture it: my anus, opening like some horrific flower, accepting of the enormous chrome bee that's drawing in silently. A glorious full moon, except in this sky the moon erupts from a pin-prick and swirls outwards, terrifying the inhabitants below as it sucks in light and air. Then it's blocked and my prerecording hitches briefly. Nothing tears, and I thank my lucky sphincter. It has been trained well through weeks of a predominantly liquid diet, punctuated with badly chewed crisps and barely digestible lumps of tough meat.

Whatever it was, it's in now, and I sag with some relief. That wasn't as bad as I was expecting. On reflection, it was nothing worse than a bit of: Oh, oh, wait, no… Hold it. Yes, alright. Over the ridge. And… safe. Nothing I can't handle or deem too high a price for continuing this investigation into determining if Ben was murdered. Though at this stage, if I find out that it was just an accident, I'm digging the bastard back up and lamping him.

Oh sweet Jesus covered in marmite and set on fire alongside suckling pigs, it's inflating. Ram is now sat on my back, the rubber crotch of her mirror-shine trousers softening with the heat of her body and sticking to me, snapping and snatching in grinding little jerks. I suck my lip, bite my tongue, gurn, anything just to not think about this.

I throw my thoughts violently to what could be happening in the next room. I read the specials available in the catalogue provided. At the big houses there's a profile on every Mistress—costumes, talents, skills, preferences, all alongside a lovely picture. Here, in Ram's personal dungeon that boasts not two but four independent rooms, the catalogue was smaller but still incredibly specific. I reason that she could have loaned out one of the two remaining rooms to her domme friends, and that they're currently doling out page fifteen: the Geek one, specifically tailored to fanboy fantasies. And not the obvious Gold Bikini one, at that. Some pasty little Geek could be tied up on a rickety chair in a hastily constructed interrogation room, water dripping and the bare light bulb swinging and flickering with dull, electrical twangs on its cord. A dominatrix dressed as Darth Vader could be looming over him, her costume modified so that the cloak sweeps about her indignant white breasts, empiric duty boots now tall and poised to pierce the backs of hands and the valley between shoulder blades.

Darth Bitch, a cane in one hand and a Force Effects Lightsabre greased up and ready to go in the other, beating on this naked little Geek screaming

"Where is it? Where is it?" over and over, the voice simulator in the helmet desperately trying to keep up with the perversity. The Geek won't have a clue as to the what, let alone the where, and his mewlings only churn his own excitement, flux capacitor-fuelled fear and potent arousal. He's so pale he reflects the light, looking like some angular fish reflected in the middle of Darth's helmet. Curved and bloated, his eyes will fixate on the pitiful image of himself, and Darth Bitch will not be pleased when she sees that his attention has deviated from her and the terror she is inflicting upon him for a mere second.

The extendable blade is threatened again, snapping in and out from its full length down to a blunt hilt with which to bludgeon. In the corner of the Geek's mind, he sees his girlfriend being playfully dragged and flogged by a Stormtrooper, then he goes on to think about the pale, awkward, elbowy sex they'll have when they're out of here. And ringing in his ears, all the way down the road, he'll hear Darth's rumbling voice screaming: "Where is it?"

My engorged arse is demanding my attention, and no amount of Star Wars BDSM fantasising can save me. It feels like I could hide a baby whale up there now, carting it safely past the Japanese officials as I hobble through the airport, then releasing it rescued and saved with an almighty sigh back into the ocean after the flight. It would look up at me from the water, greasy with lube and stained brown and magenta, its giant mouth hanging open in outraged horror; its eyes scream, "How could you?" whilst holding up its fins like they're broken to me. And I'd just smile and adjust my belt, pointing a strong finger at it, saying: "You owe me, bitch."

A wet sucking noise as I feel the inflated dildo

shrinking rapidly before popping out of me. I feel like a cave with the ceremonial burial rock dragged away from the entrance, revealing a surprisingly empty tomb inside. A wintery breeze blows deep into my crevices for the first time. That's me stretched, then.

Ram saunters around the equipment I'm tied prone to and puts on a huge, turgid strap-on at my eyelevel. I stare at the shiny veined thing in horror. I suddenly have a whole lot more respect for women. To have something like that coming at you and to still keep your ankles sailing apart and your mouth arranged in a pleasantly surprised little shape takes some doing. More lube is sprayed. I try desperately not to allow any sort of gaseous motion to take place, knowing that the results would be wet and sloppy.

I wish I'd gotten hammered for this, but then I was advised against it. It's safest to have my faculties with me at all times, like when hunting bear. Being done up the arse by a dominatrix when you don't really want to be but have to because your partner in crime fucking landed you in it is exactly like hunting bear. You're aware of the possibility of getting hurt. You're also scared of just how bad it's going to be. Your first instinct is to freeze and seize up, but the advice is to go floppy and just let them maul you about until they lose interest. Being lively spurns them on. And you smell afterwards. That's unavoidable. If you're really lucky, you might just get a pay off and end up with a smile as well as a story to possibly tell one day. But most likely not. Most likely, you're just trying desperately not to get fucked over too hard, to maintain some shred of dignity, and to survive it.

The dong comes knocking at my back door. It's narrower than the inflated dildo at full capacity. That helps. This one moves though, in a horrible pistoning motion from Ram's hips, varying between rude intrusion and digestive relief, interjected with sphincter confusion. I try to go to a Happy Place, only to find that it has fucked off and left me. I try to think of something remotely sexual, believing that at least having an erection might help me to find some source of pleasure in this. I know it's possible. Unfortunately, my efforts only end up with me envisioning the hippos and crocodiles from Disney's Fantasia taking part in a Nazi composed sexual practice, rows upon and rows of madly lit animal buttocks with rejects from the Small World ride keeping everyone in rhythm with batons. I settle for just trying not to visualize this.

I hastily return to Darth Bitch. The Geek has been released now, crawling on his elbows and stomach to reach his tortured girlfriend who's being forced to suck on the end of the Stormtrooper's gun. Her butterfly glasses have made a bid for freedom, hanging off the side of her face with one stem jabbing at the corner of her watering eye. Her hair is long, lank and without style, perfect for wrapping a gloved and plastic-armoured hand about and seizing her head with. She opens her eyes to slits, mousy grey irises shifting to her Geek, moaning about the gun, breasts slick with sweat and her own saliva. He almost reaches her before Darth Bitch mounts him like a pony, her cape covering almost the entirety of his body and her helmet bobbing as she finds her balance. The lights on her chest panel continue to flicker in their steady, programmed rhythm. The iconic breathing continues unabated and unexcited. The voice simulator maintains its heady, baritone chill, rumbling over his gasped moans and squeals of delight at being in physical contact with Darth's cat flap.

Ram isn't thrusting anymore, thank God, and I'm sure we're coming close to the end of our session. She'll be going to check on Tilley first to release her before she lets me go and I hand over a credit card. Tilley wanted to see me like this, because Tilley clearly doesn't care if she lives or suffocates to death on my balls. I hope she at least got the damn files off the computer, or all of this would have been painfully pointless.

The dong is out, and my knees buckle as I relax. That sloppy, bubbling sensation begins again, and the air seems to whistle. Then, without warning, there's something hard and cold. It flashes through my mind that she might have taken to filling a condom with water, freezing it and is now in the process of shoving it up my arse to bond unshakably with my back passage. I'd have to have, horror of horrors, a second warm enema just to get the thing back out.

Once it's up, it remains cold and hard, the edges too sharp and narrow. It doesn't hurt, but Christ, that shit ain't natural. Oh, look, it turns too. A sharp jerking motion from twelve to three. She tells me to hold it. I try to bring my lips back from where they've gone to take up residence against the gumline at the back of my teeth. It doesn't happen, but my arse remains clenched obediently. It seems to be operating independently of me now, not trusting me with its safety after all that. I make a strangled little sound, my most genuinely pitiful of the many that have been pulled out of my repertoire today, and listen to Mistress Ram leave the room.

Chapter 10

Touch Down

I am largely unconscious or otherwise isolated from my faculties for the next three days. I decided that I deserved a reward for the sacrifices I'd nobly made and needed enlightenment as to what to do next, so I'd gone out and found a questionable stranger to buy fantastical substances from. Tilley got sick of me and had vanished by the middle of the first day. I wanted to look for her, but I was terrified at the prospect of going outside as I knew it wouldn't be long before I was apprehended by the police, whom I'd end up telling absolutely everything about why we were here. Then they'd check my rectum for concealed weapons, find it bruised and puffy, and I'd be horribly embarrassed.

I spent the second day of my isolation utterly convinced that my hands were two large, endangered species of moths, and I carried them around the room in search of a substitute for their natural habitat of a mossy tree stump. I taped newspapers and cushion covers to the windows to dim the natural light and make it more like private woodland, then laid on the bed, drank heavily, and watched them flutter clumsily above me.

On reflection, I have been in far worse states than this. A few years back, I was in Ecuador researching something that warranted my being in Ecuador at the time. I happened to come upon meeting with a shaman, real power of the earth stuff, and for the price of some of my own perception altering substances, he helpfully gave my aura, and all the fuzzies connected, a cleansing. This involved him breathing deeply from a hollow log filled with smouldering plants and seeds, having me do the same, and then thumping me hard on the top of my head.

The following week was something of a blur. I was successfully restrained in my tent for the first night, during which I had some of the most fucked up dreams involving whales on stilts and bioluminescent pigs that I've had in some time. The next day, I escaped my captors and wound up in a fast river, swept downstream for a mile or two into a wet nest of bracken and a dead sloth. Baby caiman crocodiles were burying their bodies into the bloated and split torso, their tails tangled in the moss-clogged fur. I tried to adopt one but it wouldn't accept me as a surrogate, so I abandoned it to the tide and watched with vindictive pleasure as it was swept away from its siblings. There was something involving an Incan temple as well, and I may have in fact become a man-God for some time.

I would make a fearsome God, but not in England, it seems. Here, I am rapidly overwhelmed by the wet, grey and cold which makes me just want to start various small fires to make the place more interesting. However, I found that being crammed inside a hotel room with nothing but the carpet and bed linens to play with since everything else has been torn apart and affixed to the windows has been a worse experience.

On the third day of my plight, I went out and tried to find Tilley. Failing that, a substitute for Tilley would do. That is what I had now, and it had somehow turned out to be a post-op female to male transsexual. I'm not quite sure how I got it to follow me here, but I suspect that it thought I was trying to pick it up in my violently drunken way, and then came back with me to see if I was going to accidentally suffocate on my own tongue. Or drown in vomit. Or eat a mouse head. I forget what I said.

The two of us sat for a long time in the dim room just eating the little food items we'd had in our pockets, or it did at least. It seemed to have an unending supply of chocolate lurking within the slim confines of its jacket. I had fluffy mints and a wrapped chocolate éclair that was almost fossilised. Because we had nothing better to do, and we absolutely were not going to have sex, I told it everything about why Tilley and I were here. I explained about Ben's death and our suspicions surrounding it; how we'd come over here to meet the maker of the gimp hood and then gotten information from a dominatrix that the dearly departed had once visited. I didn't go into the specifics of that particular investigatory detour.

It was fairly noncommittal about the whole thing, though interested all the same. There was some back and forth before we both lapsed into silence. Now I've been sat on the edge of the bed for some time watching how it moves. It ate a Snickers loudly and eyed me. Tilley came back ten minutes ago, though I was so transfixed by the thing that I barely noticed.

"Are you going to ask me?" Tilley asks from the striped chair, emptying a multi-pack of crisps onto the floor to take out the one flavour she'll eat. She throws another pack at me and one to the confused lesbian.

I tear into the foil packaging and inhale the cloud of chemicals that puffs out, delighted at the high synthetic content of my first solid meal in days. "Ask you what?"

Tilley looks at the lamp, apparently considering throwing it at me. I'm convinced I could deflect it through cunning manipulation of the minute air currents within the room. She throws another packet of crisps at me instead, and I allow it to hit me in the face. "What I found out on Ram's computer? About Ben? Remember? The whole reason we're in this fridge-come-swimming-pool country?"

My hand flaps about a bit, gesturing for her to continue. I steal another look at It, who is watching the exchange with apparent interest. Tilley hasn't spoken to the third occupant of this foul room yet. "Whilst you were off squealing like an imploding pig, I went through Ben's profile from Ram's computer. His homosexuality was already becoming apparent back then, and he said he'd dabbled with infantilism."

Ah, infantilism. Where you get to piss yourself, garble inarticulately and "innocently" fondle women in nursing uniforms before having to suffer the indignity of old age. Tilley has told me that my catatonic days do not count as a fetish, and are merely the result of my accidental and failed attempts at killing myself through ingestion of lighter fluid and gin-soaked biscuits.

Tilley gets up to peel a cushion off the corner of the window, the weight of the foam-filled, god-awful fabric meaning that it was already sagging and pulling away. Folding herself up on it, she resumes munching her crisps. "Breath play, it turns out, was something he did express an interest in. Ram didn't do any asphyxiation play with him, but he raised it. Mostly the session they had was straightforward bondage and domination. It was the stuff from the cool down talking afterwards that seems to comprise most of her file on him."

"So, he could have actually been into it?" My words are clicks and snaps around my food, but she nods. "Which means he could have been doing it regularly with his partner, and it was either an accident with him or an accident with another Dom he was messing around with?" Another nod and I'm disappointed for some reason. I think I wanted this to be a real life murder mystery, with intrigue and twists. So far, it's been ramrod straight.

Tilley looks across to the I Can't Believe It's Not Homo in the corner. "He's filled you in on what we're doing out here, I take it?"

It sniffs and gives her a droll look. "There was some explanation in between the inarticulate screaming and demands for booze, yeah."

"I'm Tilley, by the way."

"Paul."

I wave my hand mystically. "I hereby proclaim you Butchy."

My partner in crime snorts at me. "Ignore him. His brain is comprised of scabs and alcohol soaked pig flesh."

"Makes a lot of sense. Still doesn't help me understand why you're hanging around with him."

Deciding that I don't particularly want to hear the topic of me being bitched out right now, I stand abruptly and head towards the door. I need the flesh of a young animal doused in fat and covered in mayonnaise immediately.

Chapter 11

Tilley's Chapter

Paul sends Gabe's retreating back a droll look before swinging his gaze back to me. There's a quick intelligence in there and no small amount of mirthful bemusement. His features are a little too fine to be a man's, lending an appealingly androgynous quality. There's no mistaking that particular brand of forced confidence along his jaw though. It's something I've seen the cousin of in Gabe's face a fair few times.

"So, why exactly are you with him?"

"Oh there's no *with*. We're not a couple." Apparently I lunged at the implication so fast he found it funny.

"Yeah I got that much." He fidgets, readjusts, and it's impressive that he's got that unsubtle male nuance to draw attention to his crotch down perfectly. "I mean why hang around with him all about the world?"

I swallow back the '*so I can lose him en-route*' retort, scrunching up the empty crisp packet into a tight, greasy ball. Then I shrug with the same smile I give to everyone who asks that question, or something close to it. Sometimes it's even a blunt '*how haven't you strangled him with your thighs yet?*' "He's just always around, like a bad penny or when you're having one of those days when you keeping thinking you can smell eggs."

He rumbles thoughtfully, and I'm very aware of his lack of an Adams apple. I know male-to-female can get tracheal reshaping, but is there anything available for women going the other way? Mind, it's easier to dig a hole than to build a pole, so it's an uphill battle all the way for Paul's type of transsexual. "Not even childhood sweethearts then?"

I laugh outright at that. Damn he's dogged about closeness. "Nah, nothing like that. Just partners in hijinks and misguided adventures going way back, which is pretty much what we are now."

Standing, I go over to the bed and slump back on the pillows, flicking crumbs around the bed sheets with my toes. "We've had some great nights, like standing around doing lines off a postcard outside Buckingham Palace. Things like getting on buses out of our minds with absolutely no idea where we were going but ending up right where we wanted to be." I laugh having forgotten all about the next one. "Getting the gerbils out of their cages at the pet shop and going after them with rudimentary spears. You know, kid stuff."

The memories come pouring back and I take an overly long blink, scanning over them. It was never a real mystery how I ended up tagging along with Gabe on another of his misguided wanders; every time, he just invited me and, as it was always a laugh or perversely educational, I was always up for it. I've seen and done things with him that I never would have alone, but he would. Hell, I know he's done worse. It's not that I'm a cautious person. I just have ideas and desires that feel too big or abstract to ever realise, but if an opportunity comes up with him, he's more than happy to pound down the detour and help me to achieve something of the fantasy. I've never found anyone who, when I say, '*let's borrow a flamingo and dye it blue*' will say, '*yeah, though if we do its food it'll be more natural and permanent.*'

There haven't been any detours on this one though. Gabe's got an edge of manic seriousness creeping in that I haven't seen in years, and he's barely writing. Usually the self-involved bastard is absorbed in a notebook for hours on the side of sticking his own thoughts down, but there's been almost nothing of it. It's like some fundamental fragment of this, of Ben's death and the community he was a part of, really matters to him, and I want to stick this out with him to the end to see what that is.

This is the first time a 'jaunt' has been so serious. We started out small and stupid, and then changed very little. I snort when I remember our budget outings, and the ones even smaller than those. Paul's watching me, quietly interested.

"Christ, there was this one time we were mashed or stoned or something, and I was hiding this treasured toy bear relic of his that I'd found in his flat. Hid it in the microwave, which is where he found it and went totally ape shit at me for. He demanded that I take it out somewhere and buy it drinks as an apology, so we spent the night carting this bloody malformed bastard of a toy round the city, introducing it to people and saturating it with all manner of ungodly mixers. He'd sit in the damn bars and be talking to me, and this bear would be turning its head to stare at the folk next to us. He'd be shouting at it and slapping it and apologising to them, and I'd be lacing his drink with a mild laxative just so he'd demand we go home and let us sleep the whole thing off." I might have gone too far with that anecdote and wave it off. "Stupid, inane, ill-planned stuff."

Paul nods slowly. "Sort of exactly what you've been doing now, then?"

That wasn't quite the response I had been expecting. There's something of a pregnant pause. "Come again?"

"Well you've both been complete retards, haven't you?" I assume that was a rhetorical question. "You've flown across half the fucking world to inspect gimp hoods to see if Ben could have suffocated, then gone on to find out whether or not he was into asphyxiation by having you hack his former mistress's computer, and at no point has it occurred to you to go see Carl and fucking ask what happened, and see if he lies. Occam's razor," he adds with a stabbing finger.

Sitting forward abruptly, I hold up a finger. "Actually, that's what I said way back after we left Hugh and Nora's. And you know what Gabe said? He said he wanted to draw it out, and let it be like old times."

He folds his arms, throwing up a condescending eyebrow. "You're sure about that? You sure he didn't just want to do it his way and not your way? Piss about for a few weeks, wandering aimlessly around the fetish community and risking getting into a heap of trouble? 'Cause I've spent a few hours with him now and based on that, I can tell you that it's fairly bloody likely."

My shoulders touch back against the cold headboard slowly, and I thunk my head back as I roll the notion around. "It's a theory," I announce, feeling even more dubious when I hear myself say it. "I'll run it up my flagpole, see who salutes."

Paul grunts and stands up, thrusting his hands deep into his pockets and looking around awkwardly. "I'm just saying if it were me and my money I was throwing around on it, I would have just gone straight to the obvious source and started from there."

"Oh it's not my money. It's all his. I've not paid

for anything yet, really." Quietly, the thought pipes up that maybe Gabe is dragging this out to spend more time with me. I'll drink something stout and think on that later though.

Sitting back down on the edge of the chair, Paul looks quite interested in the fact that Gabe is happily financing all of this. "Really?"

I glean the vibe, the keenness, and feel a grin sliding out. Seems Gabe's in for a surprise when he gets back.

Chapter 12

Orientation

To no surprise of mine it's raining again as I charge off into the dimming light on the hunt for a greasy take-away. Since my boots touched English soil, I've been craving a kebab, and despite having been wrecked or hung over for the vast majority of our stay so far here, I haven't gotten my hands on one of those yellow polystyrene boxes where the bottom is slowly beginning to bubble and rot through from the inside out from the grease. Fish and chips; pie and chips; a battered sausage dipped in curry sauce and dripping across gleaming golden oblongs of potato—those are real meals. A kebab has the same purpose as a deep fried Mars bar: to fulfil the gluttonous urge, fuel a syrupy belch and to slowly commit suicide. The extra salad is purely optional and purely garnish. So damn satisfying, even when you substitute the grey/brown meat for chicken with the flimsy excuse that it's marginally healthier.

I find a Turkish kebab shop and watch them shear off ribbons of Alsatian, or whatever, then nest up on one of the high stools to eat inside. There is no way I'm leaving any sooner than I have to, back to the pit of voles lying in wait at the hotel. Rather, I accelerate my forthcoming wet noisy death by putting my arteries into a similar condition to that of my liver.

It's really sinking in that I'm back in England, a country that, despite all my roaming, I haven't set a foot on in years. And rather than a scenic visit, a base-touching with old friends or just a damn holiday, I'm here chasing yet more filth and depravity for the sole purpose of feeding some gaping chasm that only the bleakest facts about the world can fill. For years I've flown the banner of 'research' and poured copious notes and transcripts into obscene books, sat with the mad and the destroyed and leached off every potent word to fund my search for more. I've set up no charities for the topics my books cover—I haven't tried to change anything. I've bettered nothing, especially myself.

I read last year about an elite squad of former SAS and military types that storm child brothels around the world, stealing the kids back and intervening since the governments won't because the kiddie-fiddlers share some of the offices. My first thought was to dig up and write about child prostitution, though I cast this aside when I realised that to go undercover I would probably have to adopt the guise of the lowest scum, which I could no more do than storm in and save them all myself. The only remote good I can claim is raising awareness, but I know that's not what people buy my books for.

Chewing down the rubbery and potent meat, I'm disgusted to find that I'm not hungry and that my psyche has found some sort of terribly clarity after the last few days of hallucinating and chattering to the wall lamps. I'm going to need a big drink later, a recurring theme recently. Taking out my journal from my inside coat pocket, I jot something akin to that as the first line on a clean page.

How Tilley keeps letting me get away with this shit I'll never know. I think she would have parted my company many years ago if she knew where and why I disappeared for months at a time, turning up again with cheques to cover all my meals and cigarettes for another year. Her tours in between those with me are far more inane and unthreatening. I don't think she could see the things I've seen. I don't know how I can see the things I do and write the things I write.

If I'd managed to stay with Laura, none of this would have happened. I shudder to think of it now, but at the time I'd have felt fine diving into a regular job that I could talk about without shuffling a bit and suddenly needing to make a phone call, something involving a shirt and a monthly payslip. Laura was good at arranging me to do everyday things like that. She cajoled my cooking skills beyond a boiled egg and anything fried, even getting me so far as to put real food in a real dish and into an operating oven. I've since returned to using the things as an extra cupboard. She didn't put up with that sort of shit and she wouldn't put up with what I get up to now. She'd probably ask me what sort of man I was to actively seek these stories out as a living, and as I can't answer that, I would have just given up and stopped.

Tilley's different though. I don't know what she would say if she found out, but she wouldn't make a judgement of my character over it, I'm certain. She might even be up for tagging along on my research trips, just like she's been up for every restless statewide pub-crawl, road trip and treasure hunt I've elbowed her into.

I'll find out after we've figured out where this investigation is going. I'm not researching a book here, but it's still important that we finish this. This is personal and over someone I know. Yet, like an albatross around my neck, I know I'm going to keep taking my notes and one day, when material is thin, I'm going to make money out of Ben's death.

Yeah, definitely need a drink. It's time to head back.

I slide the half empty box across the countertop, grunt a goodbye to the two dark men and take to the street again. It had been my intent that dodging the bitch-rant and getting a good, greasy meal instead would take my mood up to such heights that nothing would drag me down for at least a few days. Now I feel grey and washed out, like I've swallowed bleach after giving the morphine time to kick in and numb me out.

As I reach the hotel room and fumble around for my key at the door, I say a little prayer that Tilley is alone and crashing out on the bed eating biscuits and reading. Much else would send me out to buy a new bottle of scotch rather than fish out the one I've already started under the bed. Inside the room I see that Tilley is indeed on the bed, but the manliest woman in the world is still here and she seems to have bonded with it. I turn on my heel without taking my hand off the door, pulling it shut again behind me.

Tilley gets up and grabs the edge, pulling the door back open and spinning me round. She plants a hand on her hip and stares up at me. I'm deeply unsettled by this demonstration of spine, and fear that she is only a few short steps away from rigging a catastrophic device about the toilet so that when I next annoy her I will be sucked down the pipes, snap my bones up on the U-bend and be purged out into the ocean where endangered sea turtles will nibble at my pithy remains. I always did fancy being scattered at sea, though I had always assumed that my remains would have been peeled off of a dashboard and incinerated first.

"Right, we need to get in touch with Carl and arrange to meet with him, because wandering around like this is both stupid and unproductive." She arches a brow at me expectantly.

I run my tongue about my teeth, waiting for her to finish. Better to be fully equipped with the facts than face opposition with just a knowledge toothpick. "And secondly?" I take a seat on the edge of the bed, my hands playing with the key in my lap.

She grins my grin, evidencing what's been sneaking up on me for years: though I haven't hung around her enough, she's been hanging around me way too long. "Second, Paul is coming with us. And you're going to be nice about it."

When I glance to it, Butchy grins back and pulls out a cigarette. At least it smokes. I look back to Tilley and jab a finger at her chest. "You find out where Carl is, then we'll talk. I'm having a shower." Then I stand, march through into the bathroom, lock the door behind me, and mash a folded towel into my face.

As if things hadn't already been weird enough.

Chapter 13

Bugger

"You're fucking kidding me."

Tilley wasn't, her face set in grim bemusement. I slump back in the chair, still hot and prickling from the hot shower. I'd left the two of them in here whilst I'd scalded myself, shaved and taken a few long draughts of vodka whilst sitting on the toilet and mulling over Butchy's desire to be included in our strange little party. Its intentions still aren't quite clear to me, though it looks like it might have something useful to offer soon if the thoughtful expression on its face now is anything to go by.

"Seriously," she mutters, eyebrows springing briefly as she snaps up another crisp from the tiny bag in her hand. Stupid multi-packs. "Carl's in Thailand. Bangkok, specifically."

My imagination jumps to the obvious inevitably: shady, quick and busy Bangkok; more bang for your buck; white man's immunity and semen-specked money. Or maybe Carl's just got an aunt living out there. "Did you find out why?"

Narrow shoulders bounce. "No clue, but he's not due back for another week." I can tell she's guessed what I've already assumed, though she doesn't make a point to outright say it. "So what do you want to do?"

I give that a few seconds thought. "Can we get his mobile number off of someone?"

Tilley looks surprised. "You want to call him?"

Her bafflement sinks in through my pores. "No,

that'd give the game away and I don't want to just ask him over the phone. Just find out where he is."

"And if he's over there doing what you think he's doing, do you really think he'd tell you? Or at least tell you and then stay there?"

"Fair point." I exhale heavily and pick up the cigarettes from the table, coaxing one out of the carton. "I guess we'll have to wait until he gets back Stateside to question him," I reply resignedly through the first cloud of milky smoke. "I don't much see the point of wandering around a city of twenty million people, a swathe of which are renowned gougers and pickpockets."

"And yet more sweeping generalisations," Butchy mutters from across me, rolling its eyes.

It is beneath my notice at this moment in time, so I return to Tilley. "It'd be funny, yeah, and a nice cultural jaunt for twenty minutes, but I don't speak the language, neither do you, and hotel crawling for a week only to find that he's fucked off back home doesn't sound like the most productive thing to do."

Tilley's hip is already cocked and her arms already crossed in anticipation of a single brow arching. She nods to the third occupant of this hateful room. "Paul?"

"I had my gender reassignment surgery in Bangkok," he pipes up. "Spent a fair bit of time there and I'm semi-fluent. I could call around the hotels when we get there if you'll have me along."

Suspicion rises like the urge to murder in a chimpanzee. "Why do you want to come?"

It gives a half shrug. "Got nothing better to do and it's not like I'm going to have the chance to go halfway around the world to question a suspect about a dead guy again. And I can help."

The logic there is dark and terrible. I muster up my most serious 'do as I tell you' glare. "You're paying for your own damn flight."

Chapter 14

Cultural Misunderstandings

Five minutes was all I needed to form my surly little opinion of British airports, and how they were superior to American ones in only two ways: One- they are slightly better organised and, if anything, want to load you with more information than you need; Two- they are politely aggressive with their subtly placed security guards as opposed to those openly wielding large guns at you with '*just fucking try it*' faces. The far too many people qualified to have guns are the ones who shot the neighbourhood cats when they were young.

Over and around the huddled, confused grey flock of disappointed tourists and delayed businessmen is the same grim atmosphere and harsh white light that are found in all ports of flight. The fact that we're not flying back home but to some buggery-drenched country to ask a man if he killed his boyfriend is doing little to help my mood.

Tilley took the task of buying the tickets away from me immediately, along with my credit card, because I looked fit to go postal on everyone in this place, especially the children kicking out from where they were sitting on top of suitcases. No: especially the ones doing that and screaming in that rising, piercing sound that only minors can make. No, actually: especially the ones kicking, screaming and throwing bottles at the backs of my knees, who go immediately mute and blank when I turn on them with a snarl. Those would be the first to go.

Butchy was invited to go along with Tilley to the desk, but stupidly turned this offer down and lurked with me. This upset me greatly so I abandoned it for the closest café thing hoping they had alcohol. They didn't. I ordered an espresso and watched it ooze with chewy viscosity out of the machine. I'm very pleased that Butchy didn't follow me.

Because of how I look and the general ambiance about me, people of a similar disposition are somehow drawn into my orbit, like two rare birds briefly passing into each others awareness for the sake of continuing the species once a year, though that is a crap analogy as there's no way I'd have sex with anyone like me. I know where I've been and I wouldn't want any of it, nor would I want anything off the man who's just sidled up beside me even if I were turned spontaneously and flamingly homosexual.

From my side, he runs his fingers anxiously over his lips, scans over my fingers and the gentle tobacco stains, and finally speaks in a quiet, deep voice. "Want coke?" The accent is thick and rich, like an old letter with great looping words written in chunky black marker.

I neck my tiny yet strong—thus manly—coffee and grin, trying not to look too pleased. Would I like some coke for this very long flight where I shall be caged with a transsexual called Butchy whom I don't like but must rely on, whilst suffering vivid flashbacks to my unwanted and vigorous penetration by a dominatrix because the tubular shape of the plane, to me, is going to be like a bursting balloon to a Vietnam veteran, all the while only being allowed to intake tiny amounts of alcohol by the dumpy stewardesses who don't understand that standards have slipped and we now all begrudge them for slipping the shackles of their tiny, tight uniforms and flush-red painted lips? Why yes, yes I would.

My New Friend indicates to the other side of the complex where people are milling around, some excited, some weary, most in severe need of antidepressants, and we head through them all into the toilets. The Gents is huge and the urinals seem to stretch on for a mile. We go down to the bottom of the artificially fresh smelling room to the cluster of cubicles and subtly slide ourselves in one, locking the door. I immediately fumble around for my wallet, happy to see that Tilley didn't take any of the notes when she ran off with my card, and begin thumbing through them without revealing how much I've got. I can play poor and get a cheap high, particularly as it seems he's keen to get rid of the stuff.

When I look back at him with a monetary offer in mind I see that he's watching me with his trousers undone. And his penis hanging out. It's big, black and fluffy at the base. Apparently "cock" and "coke" sound remarkably similar through that accent.

"You don't happen to have any coke as well, do you?"

He looks at me blankly and sort of wiggles his dick at me. I put my wallet away, manoeuvre around him quickly to get at the door and clumsily let myself out. He follows a few seconds later, still doing up his flies, and walks past me fast enough to overtake. I notice Butchy standing at the closest urinal, away from everyone else and smirking at me.

The urge to shove the blue urinal cake down its throat is almost but not quite overwhelming. "Oh naff off." I then deliberately stand next to it to make a point that I'm completely unflustered. "What're you doing in here?"

"Taking a piss. What're you doing in here?"

I ignore that, staring intently at the wall until curiosity gets the better of me and I have to roll my head, crack my neck and take a peak. "See you got a dick in Thailand," I observe, surprised. I'd been convinced there was a sock down those trousers.

"Yeah, I'm all man in every sense of the word." His hackles are raised and I don't look back at my bit of wall, instead giving him the courtesy of a stare. "I piss like you do, I've got an M on my license just like you do, and I don't bleed, lactate or take it up the arse."

Hopefully, the 'like you do' that quietly runs through my head is purely imagined and not just uttered under his breath. His gaze is hard, challenging. I respect that. I can see why Tilley doesn't mind him. Mentally, I lift him from the "Butchy" label and do him the small honour of restoring his real name. I would need to have all my skin torn off through hours of scraping by rough bunions and corns before I'd ever confess to that out loud though. I've seen your penis, thus I have an iota of respect for you. It would go down so well.

I nod down to his crotch again, both of us done peeing though neither of us looking to move just yet. "I've gotta ask mate: what's it made of?"

Clearly Paul doesn't quite know what to make of the lack of a rebuttal and frowns before shrugging it off. "Abdominal muscle and skin from my thigh."

"How do you pee through it?"

"Urethra is stretched right through."

"Get hard ons?"

"Harder and longer than yours. Mechanically assisted, but the best I can have."

We both zip up and wander over to the sinks,

wash our hands and bend over to dry them off by grabbing at the bottoms of our trousers. I straighten, pat my ribs to make sure my wallet is still there and didn't get nicked during the whole coke/cock confusion, then look back to Paul. "Reckon we can get a beer in this place?"

He starts heading towards the door, hands working inside his coat sleeves. "Once we get the boarding passes off Tilley, we can go through into departures. There's a bar there with more than beer."

"Sounds good. I think I need some nice, normalising alcohol after all this."

Chapter 15
—
Reclined

Our seats are scattered about the plane and we were lucky to get those on the next flight out to Bangkok. Tilley takes the cancelled window seat and leaves Paul and me to randomly take one of the remaining seats further back along the plane. When we finally board, I stop off down the aisle to see who Tilley is next to. It's a lanky young man with a tall, strong nose which is currently directed downwards at the handheld gizmo in his hands, thumbs flying over the keys as he's writing on the tiny but complete keyboard. Tilley has already taken out her pillow and is leaning into it as she stares out of the window, one eye occasionally checking on me.

I lean onto the back of the kid's seat. "You know," I begin in a whisper, "I've got a seat which isn't next to one of the most famous bestial porn stars of our time."

The poor sap looks up from his gadget, sneaks a glance at Tilley and then looks back to me. "Really?" I hear Tilley sigh and thunk her head against the plastic window.

I nod. "Yeah. You mean you didn't recognise her? Patricia Pony they call her, because—"

"Alright man," he interjects as he fumbles with his seatbelt and stands, shoving his ticket into my chest and reaching around me into the overhead compartment. Once he gets his bag, I hold out my own ticket and slide down into the seat he has just so nicely vacated for me.

Tilley leans forward and takes the flight magazine out of the netting on the back of the seat in front. "You're an arsehole, you know that?" she says flatly as she savagely flicks through the first ten pages, not pausing on any of them.

I do up my belt and flick the seat into the reclined position, leaning back with a smile. "Yeah, but I'm damn good at it."

Silence falls as we listen to the growing whine of the engines, the last passengers shuffling down the narrow aisles to slot themselves in like batteries into their seats. Planes have such a queer intimacy. However you traverse the length of this flying bin, you're always running your crotch or arse against someone else or at their eyelevel, all your gaseous outputs are stored in the moulded seats to be expelled like a ruptured rubbish bin when the next passenger sits down, and you know exactly what the person who used the toilet before you did. Hell, your nose is getting an action replay as you desperately pump the soap dispenser to smear the fragrant foam about the sink in the hopes that it'll overpower the creamy brown stench. But despite all this closeness and sensory familiarity, no one speaks to anyone they don't absolutely have to unless by default of relationship during the entire, eternally long flight. The airlines even seem to know this and provide a pillow to smother ourselves into unconsciousness with and a blanket to drape over our prone bodies so we don't offend the elderly.

To my right, I note that Tilley's already started fidgeting as the plane gears up to begin taxiing. The pilot is speaking over the radio, so I lean into her shoulder to talk. "You know, I saw the weirdest thing in Cuba the other—"

"What were you doing in Cuba?" she pounces,

turning her body onto me. The distraction was desired apparently.

I busy myself with getting out my tiny bag of peanuts, still resting my shoulder against hers. "Updating my terrorist watch-list profile."

"You're on the list?"

I can't believe she actually sounds surprised. "Of course. Don't you think you are? Or anyone who's been anywhere near America recently?" I resist the urge to pat her head in a condescending manner as there's a strong possibility she'd bite me, and it's cleaner to get chewed on by a donkey than to receive a bite from the human mouth. "Poor naïve creature."

She narrows her eyes before rolling them and sighing, her way of telling me to continue. This time there's actually a genuine thread of irritation in the exhalation, which is unusual and unsettling. "Go on then, what happened in Cuba?"

I plough on anyway, hoping to redeem myself through making her smile. It usually works. "I was walking around smoking a cigar, because that's like the law in the evenings there, and I stopped by this big crowd that had formed around this café. So I go through to the front to see what's going on, predicting murder, intrigue or dubious sexual escapades, and there's this big guy taking lizards—iguanas—out of boxes with small bits of furniture.

"He takes out this little love seat, those fainting couch things, and he puts the lizard on it and I swear to God, this thing reclined on it and just posed for ten minutes whilst we all took photos. An iguana reclining on a purple fainting couch."

Tilley looks like she wants to look out of the window but smiles and nods tersely to me instead. "Yeah, that sounds pretty cool."

My bag of peanuts finally open, I slip a salty treat into my mouth and move it swiftly to sit up between my cheek and my teeth. "The guy said it takes him about three months to train them to do it, but it's really worth the time. His cap was getting filled with coins. You could charge for that sort of show."

A rumbled sound of agreement this time and now Tilley does look out of the window. The plane's rolling backwards and coming about, lining up to get into the queue to take off. Her thin fingers tap the tip of the armrest violently.

My tongue retrieves the peanut and I put in another one to keep it company as I think. There have been too many shocks to my precarious mental system to think of something to say now. Worst than that, she still looks a bit pissed off with me for the whole bestiality tactic.

I sit back now that the pilot isn't talking anymore and it's just the attendants holding up seatbelts and smiling big, glossy smiles as they demonstrate the technical challenges of slotting a slip of metal into the one gap it could possibly go into. They do the same thing with the life-jackets, and I wonder if a more realistic demonstration would be more useful so that when the time comes, we're not all dumbfounded by their screams and twisted faces and can get on with saving our own sorry arses.

I sit back again though continue to watch Tilley's cheek tighten and tic. "Look, about what happened back then, I'm sorry. Didn't mean to piss you off."

"It's okay. I've come to expect it." A sardonic look beneath a raised eyebrow. "Like getting food poisoning from service stations."

That doesn't entirely fix it but the tension seems to ease a bit. I eat another peanut and look out the window around her. We're lined up for the runway now and the engines have begun to drone loudly.

Tilley stiffens and I rock into her shoulder, getting her to look at me again. "Tell me something about yourself." Not inspired, but ill-thought efforts usually aren't.

She blinks owlishly. "Like what?"

I shrug, helpless, which is nothing new. "I don't know, anything."

There's another silence but when the plane begins to hurtle forward, she gets what I'm doing and latches onto the idea. "I don't know. All the interesting stuff you already know, because you were there."

"Alright, something from further back then. When you were a kid." I make a point to talk over the engine roar and the sound of the tray tables vibrating.

Her eyes slide upwards as she thinks back, neurons firing to the right, then she smiles. "When I was really little, I used to think that all the land floated on the sea, like ice, and that the beaches sort of tapered out to nothing under the water, and that earthquakes happened when whales bumped their heads on the bottom of the land."

I pull out my sick bag and shake it at her a little. "That's so cute I may actually have to use this." She flushes and dips her chin into her collarbone. "What about volcanoes?"

Her response is a few seconds coming. "Them hitting these rubbery sacks of lava stored underneath, like bubbles."

I am genuinely delighted by these answers. "That's brilliant. Wish I had something interesting like that from childhood."

The engines abruptly hit a new gear and the whole

bulk seems to tip back as we finally leave the ground. Tilley grabs my hand and clenches her eyes shut as I feel my stomach lurch. This isn't the first time she's clutched my fingers, but for once, I squeeze her hand back.

Chapter 16

The Inevitable Flashback

I've tried not to be the nostalgic, predictably habitual type, but somehow I had found myself migrating to the gravestone before which Mum and Dad were piled on top of each other in coffins that were shamefully cheap. They weren't quite pine boxes, but there simply wasn't the money for anything good. I'd wanted to get a good headstone, so something had to suffer.

It looked pretty wretched, with the twisting tree that overhung the white slab turned completely brown and covered with fat spiders centralised in hopeful webs. I had burned them off with my lighter and stamped out the small fire that rapidly emerged, figuring that the ash would do the ground some good. There were no flowers and I had to rearrange another gravestone and take one of their plastic funnels to put the ones I had brought in. I didn't know what was fitting for a two year anniversary, so I'd brought yellow roses because they were never a stranger in the house.

I didn't know what to do after I'd messed around with the flowers and water, and desecrated another grave a little bit, and talking to the cold stone didn't appeal in any way. My son's duty satisfied, I had decided that I'd done the good deed for the day and that it was time to be very selfish and get very catatonic in a very short space of time. The nearest pub was only too happy to take my money off me.

Tearing up the moist bar mat and peeling apart

the paper wafers, I stare dimly into my glass and watch the ice melt. My hands and their slow, clumsy movements send bleary colours across the round cornered cube, dark and restless. I don't notice the figure sliding onto the stool next to me until she coughs, then all I see is her hair. It's orange, but not the ginger orange that looks genetically stolen from squirrels to warrant a childhood of mocking. Orange like if all the things that were orange in the universe were melted together and poured onto her head. Her eyebrows are dark and arched. I think she's a dark blonde, really. Maybe she's trying to hide the dumb label, or maybe she's hiding something else entirely.

She's got too much eye makeup on which makes her gaze watery and sullen, which I don't reckon it's meant to be. "Doesn't look like you're having the best day," she comments, which is brave of her. "Too nice a day to be looking that miserable."

I don't know what to say to that, but we're both saved an awkward silence when the barman comes to make a cursory inspection of her breasts, which are nice in profile, and to take her order. She asks for a Jack and Coke, taking out a cigarette whilst fiddling with coins in her other hand. The smell of the smoke sets off my own monkey, and I fish out the carton from an inside pocket.

Finally, she has her drink and doesn't look to be going anywhere, though she isn't looking at me anymore. I leap. "I'm Gabe."

Somehow this delights her and she turns to face me, grinning. She holds out a hand, which I take. "Tilley. Nice to meet you." My scalp is suddenly fascinating to her, and out of spite I eye hers. There are splotches of orange and her clumsiness is strangely endearing.

Her eyes click back to my face when we part hands. "You know, you'd look better if you cut your hair short."

I don't quite know what to do with that, but the honesty is appreciated. "I didn't think it was that long."

Her nose folds up like an accordion, gently squeezed. "Yeah, it's not bad. But it'd look better short. Bring out your features a bit more." My blank stare finally registers and she blinks slowly, her mouth sagging. "Sorry. I was just thinking out loud. I do that." She looks away, chin sinking into her collarbone. "Probably shouldn't."

I grunt a little and she looks back, wary. Taking mercy and a long drag, I sit watching her through my smoke. "So what do you do, Tilley?"

A thin elbow jerks up on the edge of the bar to prop her head, and she exhales up into her fringe. "I'm a literature student."

Now I knew it, I thought I could smell the tang of books about her. "Oh right. How's that going for you?"

She half coughs, half snorts and pulls a face. "Crappy. It's gotten crappier recently with things falling to shit elsewhere." A sip, deep like mouthwash. "Nothing better for an exam than finding your boyfriend fucking your flatmate, but never mind." She toasts me. "Cures all ails."

I raise my glass as well and we touch rims. Then she lies in wait of my spleen, and I decide that not only do I like her enough to spill it but I don't care enough about how she'll react to feel censored either. Like petrol on a fire. "Two year anniversary of my parent's deaths today. Murdered at the same time so they can have the same plot, which is alright." I want to say that it's cheaper on the flowers but restrain myself.

It's interesting to me that a grimace doesn't look as alien on Tilley's face as it does on most people's. "Shit, sorry to hear that." She takes a mouthful of mixer and I do the same, then she seems to mull over my words. "You know, I really don't get what you're supposed to do at graves," she explodes, looking off at the corner of the bar. "I mean, you stand there with your flowers or whatever, and you lay them down all pretty like, and then what? Do you talk to them? Sit down in the grass and tell them how your week's been? Do you cry? Do you sing to them until you choke if it's their birthday? And on Christmas, do you tell them what you would have gotten them if they hadn't died? Tell them you saw something that made you think of them, and that it just made sense and you so wished they could be back just long enough to give them that thing because it was so right?"

"I don't know." I feel like a fish on a hook that just got swallowed whole from behind by a shark. No anger, no sadness, just a general feeling of 'what the fuck happened there?' "You ever had someone you knew die?"

Her eyes blow over me and she takes a drink blindly. "No." It's like I asked a stupid question. A pregnant pause, as some people would say, and this seems to irritate her immensely. "So what're you going to do now?"

Shaking off the frown from that sideswipe takes a second, and I buy time with a calculated thoughtful drag. "What, you mean like the future?"

She licks her lips and shakes her head. "No, I mean like this afternoon. Tomorrow. What're you going to do with yourself?"

I hadn't thought much beyond the bottom of this glass, which I intended to fill when I got there, so I ended up pulling an idea out of my arse. "Might catch a bus somewhere. Coventry maybe, or London. Just get a change of scenery."

Tilley grins, approving greatly. "That's a good idea. Hell, I could do with getting away for a bit. Mind if I come with you? Doesn't really matter where we're going so long as we can smoke and drink."

Her priorities endear me to this notion and suddenly I like my fabricated idea. "Yeah sure. Nothing like a merry adventure with a stranger."

She punches me lightly in the shoulder, her nose crinkling in a way that's far too much like Laura's nose crinkle. I fell in love with that crinkle. "We've got names, so we're not really strangers. It could be fun; roaming around for a bit away from the shit we've got on locally."

Stubbing out my dog-end, I feel the corners of my mouth twitch and the clench across my shoulders beginning to come loose. "Alright, we'll finish up and head down to the station."

After a few seconds, Tilley slaps her hand on the bar top as a revelation hits. "Oh, you didn't say— what do you do?"

"I'm a writer." That was half true. I was working on it.

She sits back, teeth exposed and gleaming. "Excellent. I've always wanted to hang out with a writer."

* * *

Tilley's asleep, half her face covered with the black eye mask she paid too much for in the airport, and most of the plane has joined her in a cold slumber. I look from my journal to her face again, running my fingers over the subtly textured pages whilst my pen balances and tips between two fingers. Strangely aware of the chill in the artificial air, I reach over and pull her blanket about her shoulders and secure it behind her with a few slow pushes. I don't wake her, thankfully, but just in case I go back to staring at my journal for half a minute afterwards.

I don't know why I suddenly got to thinking about how we met. It's not like now is the anniversary of my technically becoming an orphan, as that was five months ago and I have the blessed reverie of the next seven months to psyche myself up for it again. I've got a horrible thought that it was squeezing her hand when we took off that did it. We don't touch hands often, but I remember how obvious it was on the coach ride to London that she wanted to hold my hand and to tell me how sorry she was for me. Instead, thankfully, she just talked crap with me and bitched about the weather, which was so much better.

For my part I must have done something right, because she stayed in close contact for months afterwards until we were just seeing each other regularly and taking little jaunts to wherever we fancied. I think she got hooked on my bored, restless and investigative wanders around the country, which scaled up to the world when I got a budget to work with. Travelling wasn't anything she'd done before because she didn't want to do it alone, and I made it an easy and interesting ride. Sort of like now, actually.

I close my journal and drop it back into the bag between my feet, feeling out my own blanket and unfolding it across my lap. Tilley and I have been roaming around together for so long now, I hadn't realised that her company had become an intrinsic part of it. When I did go somewhere for the sake of a book and she didn't come, there was an absence that I put down to my underlying and constant subconscious knowledge that I was working. But I'm twigging that it's because as much as she's become addicted to seeing the world and all its peculiar curiosities, I'm becoming addicted to having her stand next to me.

Tucking the blanket around myself and running my hand over my cold nose, I try not to think about how unnerving a realisation that is. It's a damned ugly thing to know when I know that one day my finances are going to shrink so there's only enough for me to go around and she'll lose her free tickets, which means she probably won't come. It seems I've become something of a slave without my knowing, which is a nasty thought when you're sober and flying to Thailand. Or maybe, hopefully, this is sobriety talking. I decide to sleep through as much of what's left of this flight as possible and then mull it over when my brain is sufficiently cushioned with alcohol.

Chapter 17

Heat

It's like stepping through a portal to leave a grey and oppressive port, flying numb and almost catatonic for hours, and then emerge on the other side in another time and another world. The Bangkok airport is vibrant and far too lively for my soggy brain to comprehend all at once, so I take myself aside from the body of disembarking travellers and lean against the hot wall with my eyes closed. The chatter of foreign tongues, of strangely placed stresses and tonal variations, is musical and invigorating. I open my eyes and look around for the universal no-smoking sign. Not seeing one, I take out my cigarettes and light that first beautiful, wondrous smoke that almost leaves me in a state to be banned from working with children and the elderly.

"You're such a bitch to those things," Tilley's drawl drifts in. I blow smoke in her face and see from her twitch that she wants one too. Difference is, she isn't so devoted that she can't wait until she gets outside, unlike me. I'm just special.

Paul comes up behind her, readjusting his shoulder bag. The fact that he could pack for this indeterminably long stay inside one duffel is a testament to his masculinity. It has become a ritual to go through Tilley's packed and barely-closed bag for her to preen out the unnecessary. Our nominated guide for the city pulls out his phone, absently turning it on. "Did you want to go to Information and find a hotel, or are you alright just going to the one I stayed at?"

I continue to have oral sex with my cigarette. "What are the facilities?" Translation: Does it have a bar?

He rubs at his face, marred by the weariness that comes with plane-sleep. "Got a bar, showers, bit of room service and phones. Should cover what we need well enough. And it's cheap."

Well, those are the main criteria fulfilled. "Is it bearable though? Is it somewhere we can stay for twenty hours waiting for a phone call?"

"I spent three weeks pretty much entirely in one of the rooms wrapped up tighter than a drum and whacked out on painkillers. So yeah, I think it'd suit you fine enough."

It seems I've become unnervingly transparent to newcomers, like paper turned shiny and glassy because of batter grease. "We'll set up camp there, then, if that's alright with Tilley."

Tilley has given up on waiting to go outside since we've started talking and is lighting up a crisp smoke. She's surprised at the invitation of her opinion and exhales too quickly, trying not to cough. "Yeah, fine by me. Let's get out of here though. I want to see me a lady boy."

Ah, pretty Asian eye-candy. It's not just for men with an Oriental fetish anymore. Now these exotic lands are primed for that specific desire for young men so feminine that they have become totally unthreatening in almost every subconscious and primal sense of the word. They are essentially androgynous teenage girls with penises, satisfying the want of women who don't buy into the ruggedly handsome manly-man that the Western world is still trying to force down everyone's throats as the ideal and only brand. This quirky desire bodes well for me as though I am rugged, I am not manly. I don't even have a respectable belly despite absorbing enough yeast and grain to piss beer. Hell, Paul is more butch than I am, with his close-shaved head and obsessively worked on but carefully lithe physique. It interests me that Tilley has a penchant for this 'boi' breed, though I studiously do not follow this thought any further.

Paul fidgets the straps on his shoulder again and sets us off, leading us through the airport. Tilley and I follow with only half an eye on where he's going, skimming over the bright cloths, tight trousers and animated faces of this apparently happier climate. Our guide doesn't miss this. "You guys want to go out and see the city a bit whilst I call around and try to find out where this guy's been staying? Bangkok's got an amazing nightlife, and it's dead easy getting around on the Skyrail and the Metro."

I exchange a quick glance with Tilley, and I know that to say no would be like kicking a three-legged puppy in the face. "Sure, yeah. We'll do the touristy bit and get our bearings. Hopefully we'll have some leads by tomorrow morning and we can get going with the gritty stuff."

Tilley bounces in that rag-doll way that I don't see in her very often anymore, genuinely very excited to be here. It gets easy to forget that she's a bit younger than me and likes to fall into her gangly limbs and prat around sometimes, though those times have been getting thin on the ground lately. She could use a holiday more than me, it seems. I've been around this side of the world before but I left her behind on those particular trips, and I'm glad that she's only going to be seeing hotels and bars at this rate. With any luck, we'll find Carl lounging in a casino surrounded by button-nose, giggling girls with his arm around a rent-a-boy he's taking comfort in for the time being, gambling away the grief. Questioning over poker could be very fun. Very James Bond.

I quite fancy the idea of myself in a slick suit with a sexy drink, crooning smugly whilst Tilley drapes across my shoulders like a fine shawl in her low-backed gold dress. Carl would need to smoke fat cigars for that scene to really come off though. And wear a monocle. More dubious men need to wear monocles.

Mine would have to be made of brass and framed with a rubber seal, oxidising as it aged with me.

Chapter 18

—

Formica

Bangkok looks like it was given a budget ten years ago, promised that once they got developing it would keep coming, and then got cut off and returned to developing third world status after two years. The city did discover power, though, and has mated it crudely with the native technology. The few rickshaws that still potter around the streets have had bike engines put into them, so now they groan and cough with rustic charm at the tourists. The 'bum boats'—long wooden sticks with a splinter taken out in which is wedged a small person—have car engines grafted onto their rudders. Much to my disappointment, they do not race or perform high speed manoeuvres.

We leave Paul at the hotel and take a brief tour of the city to orientate ourselves and get a feel for the place. Carl is somewhere within these massive confused borders, and I like to know a place as well as I can before starting a manhunt. I get a pretty damn good overview of the place from an old man hovering by a bar doorway, who grabs my arm and offers: "Massage with kissy kissy. Wife can watch." Tilley wants us to go, but 'it'd by funny' doesn't cut as a good enough reason with me. Then there are all the girls who fire Ping-Pong balls out of their crotches like moist cannons. It's such a common entertainment practice that now they're using quirky gimmicks to try and compete.

Like New York, Bangkok never sleeps and threatens to melt our retinas with its eternal neon glow. In some areas, most of the buildings spill out into the street and clash with the market stalls that perpetually populate a huge proportion of the kerbs and corners. Most of it is food, smelling clean and oiled, scintillatingly happy in wide pans and bubbling on hot plates. Tilley insists that we stop at every single one to look at what's on offer, though neither of us are brave enough to commit to a meal just yet. The plastic-wrapped plane food is still an uncomfortable digestive memory for us both, and we are anxious at the prospect of further provoking our stomachs with something foreign and rich.

This is why McDonalds seems such a perfect venue for our first meal in a strange land. It's a prestigious dining experience out here, with white iron furniture laid around patio tables outside and big leafy plants looming over every table inside. Ronald himself greets us with a plastic smile as we go inside, his eyes painted into half moons and his giant yellow hands moulded in prayer as he bends in a bow. The menu looks almost the same as its American counterparts. Tilley gets nuggets and I greatly enjoy demanding a Samurai Pork Burger, though what's warrior about it I don't understand.

We sit down at the back of the place and unpack our greasy, comfortingly familiar meals. It's good to know that it's steadily becoming impossible to be more than ten miles from a McDonalds in any built up area. When man goes to the moon en masse to visit Disneyland Lunar, where you are tied to the rides and whirl about in the low gravity like a balloon escaping from a car window, there'll be a McDonalds ready to fill you with sugar and salt for your trip back home. The neon lights and pasty zombie server would bring the comfort of home right to your moon rock table.

Tilley's face lights up as she fans her chips out and suddenly she's stroking our Thai table. "They've even got Formica tables here!"

The Lunar tables would have to have Formica tops as well, it seems. I bite into the dark meat, sitting back a little to give Tilley room if she decides to initiate intercourse with the furniture. It'd be an entertaining evening show.

She bites the end off a chip, resting her chin in her palm and looking at me dreamily. "The first really erotic story I ever read was set in a fast food place. These two Italian guys pulled this woman in out of the rain, seduced her, and then had their way with her on the Formica tables. It went on and on about these tables, and it's just stuck with me."

I have to stop myself imagining Tilley having sex on this table. "How long ago was this?"

Another chip-tip. "A while ago. I was about twelve when I read it."

"Ever done it?" Would you like to? Honest to God, I'm going to choke myself with this porky bitch in a minute.

"Nah. Just one of those fantasies that you know you'll never do, but think about every now and then." Mashing a new chip into a little pot of barbecue sauce, she gives me a weird look. "Guess I'll have to find a guy who can pull strings to get into a place after hours."

My burger's gone and I tear the paper off my straw, hoping that Pepsi will get rid of this weird sick feeling. "Or settle for a food minion who has the keys."

Tilley doesn't say anything, staring off at the

food counter and watching the guys carrying red trays with appraising eyes. I ignore this activity with such energy that I actually jerk when my phone starts vibrating. It's Paul.

"If you guys are done, I know where Carl is. You need to come back to the hotel."

Hanging up, I see that Tilley is already up to fetch a brown paper bag after recognizing my work face. I hadn't expected results this quickly and really should have talked schemes and back-up plans with the two of them at the hotel this morning. Never mind though. I'm sure it's nothing we can't handle.

Chapter 19

So

Miles out of Bangkok, I don't know the name of this place, and I don't want to. That's nearly a lie actually, a platitude I'm telling myself to feel like a better man when the writer in me is aching to work this place and its people over like whores for the sake of meal tickets. It's not out of guilt over wealth or any other Western conscience disorder. If it was, I would have contented myself with the intention of donating to charity when I got home: a fiver a month for people to buy goats with until I lost interest in the idea or my agent decided no more advances or royalties until I shat out my next book, wrapped it nicely and sent it to him.

Tilley and I did alright following Paul past oxen and tin roofs up until we hit the point where the neighbourhood changed, and then the feel of the dark eyes of the locals studying us from the glassless windows became a greasy burn. It was evident that some money was coming in here, and the revenue sources of these tired buildings came running out of their dark doors, going straight for Paul and I and grabbing at our crotches with small dirty hands. Tilley clutches my arm and hitches with shock and borderline tears. Batting the children's groping hands away, I feel similarly sickened. We'd joked about this shit when the word "Thailand" first came up. Didn't that just bite us in the fucking arse.

Paul retreats back to where we've stopped, and

it's obvious he feels the same way. Children's hands on his recently new and expensive penis make him nervous, apparently. "Honestly Gabe, I didn't know this was going on here. I thought it'd be on the other side of the city."

I feel Tilley's fingers twitch and it makes me snap off a bit. "Where were you taking us?" I know my anger is misdirected and addled. I don't really want to hurt the kids pushing for sex and trying earnestly and clumsily to arouse me in the hopes that I'll give them money. I don't even want to punch Paul for not warning us. I'm quite preoccupied with the knowing dread of what we're going to find with Carl here, and Tilley's long-boned fingers turning into a tourniquet around my arm.

Manoeuvring his body in to make us a triangle, Paul steps close enough towards me to block the groping hands, restricting the children to our legs and arses. He answers with grey words. "I got given the name of a hotel, the hotel out here. At least now I know why I had such a hard time finding where he was staying."

Tilley sums it up for us all. "Fuck." She releases me and crosses her arms high and tight across her chest, flinching at the children and looking at me as if asking to take her home. "Fuck."

My sentiments exactly. I can't decide which I want more: to take all the kids away and leave them crippled with memories or to kill them all and know they're not here. Standing and having the reality touch hopefully is enough to make us sick.

I shuffle closer to Tilley, my shoulders rising tight to my neck. "Do you want us to send you back to the hotel and we'll carry on?" They have, mercifully, begun to give up now.

She considers it but then shakes her head instead, grim. "We've all come this far. I want to see it through, then we can go home."

I take her hand and run my thumb over her cold fingers. It's a fact that became known to me from camping with her in a crap tent in the middle of winter that all of Tilley's extremities are freezing cold. It's a mystery of medical science how a supposedly warm blooded creature can have such cold hands and feet. My hands are always hot.

Paul's watching me, the nominated leader. I finally look at him. "We keep going. Lead the way."

* * *

The hotel radiates grim presence like the house of an infamous murderer or the moors where tortured and strangled children were dug up. I'd expect to hear something from outside: screams, groans or the unmistakable rhythmic slap of flesh on flesh, but it is quiet. Everyone walks by oblivious or blanking, and I wish we could join them. We'd already decided that it would look incredibly suspect if the three of us went in together, so I volunteered myself. Tilley and Paul could wait outside, buy some food from a street vendor and try not to look like the tourists who deliberately, and knowingly, come here, then we'd all go back to Bangkok and get horrendously ratted in the dim hope that we can bleach away the whole damn day. From numerous wholehearted attempts to drink away select brain cells in the past, however, I already know it won't work. Still, there's a lot to be said for trying.

I don't take my Dictaphone in with me and I'd already decided that today wouldn't get any notation in my journal. I will not write this book.

I step through the doorway without knowing what to expect. Anticipating cool shadows and the sounds of humping people shaking through the walls of the tall, narrow staircase, I am taken aback by the receptionist. This was still technically a hotel, I suppose.

"I've got a mate staying here." Her slanting eyes blink politely. The corners of her mouth have collected white gunk. "I'd like a room with all the facilities." I want a smoke. "All the extras." I have no fucking clue what I'm doing.

"You an American?" she drawls in a high voice. The spittle stretches and snaps.

"Near enough, yeah."

A demure smile that I've seen aped better in harlots. "You pay American money?"

When I take out my wallet my hands are shaking. I force a stupid grin which cracks my face. "Sorry, I've never done this before. It's exciting, you know?"

She stands and takes two notes, vanishing them away into a locked metal drawer behind the desk. I see they can take cards as well, but I don't want any records of this. "You follow me now." Then she leads me through the door behind her. I'm passed onto someone else, a man as appealing as yellow snow, and the receptionist returns to the crude front desk.

Another door, and I get a queasy premonition of what's through it before his fingers touch the handle. I suck my tongue and focus on the metallic burn that springs up from the bottom of my mouth. I have to go along with this. Christ knows if it's worth it anymore, but every other option just got locked away behind me, and now there's a room full of children.

They're all silent and watching me passively, but I see judgement. Some of the older girls are playing parent, holding toddlers against their chests. These aren't anything like the ones on the streets. They aren't whoring out as an extra income for their families. I'm looking at business. Orphans. Bombing the place would be as much an act of mercy as retribution.

"Which do you want? Boy or girl?" He sounds impatient and rocks on his feet, folding his thick arms across his chest.

Back to the carpet of busted mattresses and the prepubescent menu. Carl would have gotten a boy. I point out the shyest one I can see, figuring that I might as well give the kid a break. "That one."

The guy goes and fishes him out, beckoning me to a side door. "He's a good one. You go upstairs and second door on left. One hour, then he comes back down and you pay again for another one." Or I can dial # and order a club sandwich.

I'm not surprised when the boy starts up the stairs first, leading me to the right room. The sheets are grey but clean, no doubt yanked off and dunked in hot water straight after each client is done.

The boy starts to pull off his t-shirt and I tear it back down onto him before falling back on my arse at the edge of the bed. I clutch my skull. I'm in and Carl's here too somewhere, fucking one of the kids. My own kid's looking quietly puzzled but determined, and because I'm sat down he tries to kneel between my feet, small hands reaching for me. I grab his arm and pull him to sit next to me, shaking my head at him. There's no point in trying to speak English to him.

The boy obviously doesn't know what to make

of the fact that I am neither buggering nor sucking him off, and he soon clams up against the headboard. Sat in silence, I offer him an éclair I find in an inside pocket, which he refuses, before I go back to just thinking.

Long minutes pass until footsteps going past the door get me onto my feet, and I open the door enough to peer past the recoiling paint on the walls. I've only met Carl once, but the memory rises up like a creature from the swamp. I catch his face in profile, his mouth wet and shiny amidst his short beard. My luck is spectacular. I'm a fucking star.

Leaving the kid on the bed, I follow Carl out. No one we pass makes eye-contact or speaks to us. He notices me once I fall into step with him outside, and thank fuck – there's a flicker of recognition. He grins, post-shagged and good naturedly. "Hey, never fancied I'd be seeing you here."

Tilley and Paul aren't where I left them, but that's looking to be for the best. If I just play along, I can get him talking over drinks and post-buggery nibbles. The subject of Ben is bound to come up. "Yeah, you get all walks round here. Where're you headed now? I just got here yesterday and I don't know the best places to get lunch yet."

He laughs and claps me on the shoulder with a hot hand. I so very much want to throw up into his open mouth. "There' a place a little way out. I wouldn't mind the company."

This all seems to be going suspiciously well. We come about the building and start down the shady alley that will lead us onto the main dirt street. Carl keeps chattering away to me, trusting me as like-minded because, hell, why else would I be at the same child brothel that he's, coincidentally, also patronizing, other than to buy sex? It couldn't possibly be because I've flown halfway round the world steadily painting a picture of his possible guilt, before getting a tip-off from my FtM transsexual tour guide that the suspect I've been pursuing to interview is in this notorious area. No, absolutely not. I'm confident I'll get the measure of truth in his answers, no trouble. It's already feeling a bit suspect that despite the fact that he recently lost his long time boyfriend in a freakish accident, he's as right as rain and happy as Larry. However happy Larry is.

The banshee cry from behind us might as well be the universe's way of telling me I'm kidding myself to think it could all go this smoothly. Tilley's launched into Carl's back before Paul can stop her, and then there's the wet crack of his skull hitting the stone wall.

Bollocks.

Chapter 20

Red

I've seen Tilley cry before, usually after she's turned herself into a wine bag or when I've hurt myself spectacularly and she's just laughing that damn hard. But I've never seen her cry like this before, swelling and shaking on her knees with rage. The shoulder of my shirt is damp.

Paul's reacting the worst of us, though. I could see the woman there when he hitched and shook, wrung and held his hands against his chest and throat. Many children find it a huge comfort to hold their genitals when frightened, but he went for the empty space where his breasts used to be. Hunched over and eyes everywhere, he trembles violently in the stillest position he has held in the last few minutes. "What now? What do we do now?"

A deep, dry swallow and he sets his jaw, watching me. He has to be a man. He had a year as a woman living as a man, and had to ingrain inflection and attitude into every action. Cracks appear in every personality, genuine or fabricated, when pressured like this though. They've done experiments to determine that.

My arm is starting to cramp from holding Tilley against me so tightly, and my thighs aren't doing much better. "Well, it's a result."

That's clearly not what he wanted to hear, though it's sort of correct. Carl did kind of confess under the barrage of Tilley's screamed demands and obscenities. It was probably the truth, too, given that being concussed and pummelled in the face aren't the best conditions for fabricating lies. The sod's a bit too dead to contradict us now, anyway.

Tilley shudders, grabs her head as if her mind is dribbling out of the pores in her scalp. "What the fuck am I going to do now?" Her first words in a long while, and they're far from calm.

Paul squats between us and Carl's body, crumpled and cooling against the wall. He's still fidgety, and I know he's only joined our level because it's a position he hasn't adopted yet, and it might feel better. "We've got to get out of here." There's a line of hysteria, feeling as a woman and a man and demonstrating more rawness than Tilley and I. Shitstorms are a touch newer to him than us, though murder is a novelty to us all. "Sooner or later someone's going to look down here."

I don't help. "And knowing my luck it'll be the one trigger-happy cop or soldier around here."

A despairing rush of air from him and Tilley shakes her head, pulling away from me. "We've got to tell someone. I have to hand myself in." When in trouble and doubt, be a good girl.

I grab her but stop short of actually shaking her. "Not a chance. Do you have any idea what they'd do to you?" My imagination throws it all at me at once, and the barrage is worse than what I just saw her do. And there'd be nothing I could do to save her from it.

She can't see past the now to that though, her teeth bared and the joints of her hands turned white. "He's dead, Gabe!"

Oh yes, she'd just have to scream that bit, wouldn't she? I stand and start dragging her down the alley. Paul follows because he doesn't want to be alone with the body and seems grateful when I stop in the sun and swing my attention onto him. "You said we should get out of here, so we're going to. I'll try and calm Tilley down. You go."

He nods at the straightforward task. "I'll find a taxi." Then he takes off down the road, single-mindedly and no doubt chanting not to look back. I wouldn't blame him if he took that taxi for himself and left us.

My hand begins to move in long, instinctual ovals about Tilley's spine as we walk, and she speaks into my collarbone between hitched breaths. "I'm not like you, Gabe. I can't just write this off."

That stings far more than I could ever admit. "You're right, you're not like me. You're better off, and that's why it hurts so much." The pressure from inside the alley follows us like a cartoon cloud. "But he wasn't exactly a shining example of humanity. Not only did he fly out here to have sex with kids, but he staged his partner's death when he got found out." I really should have seen that coming, with it being nearly as obvious as the old butler did it cliché. "Thing is though, the shit you do and see starts to feel less like a kick in the face and more like a bruise the more time passes and the longer you have to come to peace with it." I follow on with a private tone, as if she wasn't the only one listening. "Bonus here is I think he deserved it, and the way I've been feeling, I might have done it myself at some point."

I see a taxi rumbling up the road, probably the same one that brought us out here. Tilley forces the heels of her hands across her face, breathing in stiffly through her nose. "Can you take me home now?"

I lick my thumb and wipe away the worst smears of mascara beneath her eyes. "Yeah, but we're gonna stop off in England for a bit first. Think I know somewhere that'll help."

Chapter 21

—

Placebo

Not everyone cries at funerals. Television and film have been lying to us for years. It's not just the surly anti-hero who doesn't weep amongst the veils, either. There's standing room only at this service and as more mourners speak, it becomes concrete to Tilley and I that Michael Alans was quite a decent guy. But we have never heard of Michael Alans before now.

Tilley's fingers pull pressure about mine and I lean my ear to her. "I'm done if you are."

We slip out of the small church and light cigarettes amongst the graves. Someone has shuffled a card deck nervously around here and dropped it. The wind's spread them about the headstones, and I pick up the five of hearts from freshly turned soil.

"How're you doing?" It's the simplest question I have that comes to mind.

Tilley's been uncharacteristically quiet since I elbowed her out of Bangkok through various implorations and threats. We parted ways with Paul this morning at the airport, and he'd wished me good luck. At the time I didn't know what for, but I'm beginning to get an idea.

Hands fisted in her pockets, Tilley's whole body is tight around itself. "Doing okay." Even her voice is worn and stilted. I've never wanted to do good for another person more than I do now, but the best thing I can think to do is keep holding her hand and lead her through the rows of headstones.

Ben's grave is fresh and faintly putrid, all the flowers from his funeral starting to decay as their stems turn to mush in the stagnant water cones. Only the handmade leather roses continue to stand erect, their rusty hue looking like burns against the white stone. They might be from the seller we met at the Other Country Market, who may still be under the impression that he murdered him with the hood he made. We know better, and sooner or later, I'll get around to telling him otherwise.

"I'm glad we couldn't go to his funeral."

I feel a moist warmth building between our palms. "You mean now we that know what really happened?" Hindsight's a wonderful thing if you've got the stomach for it.

"About Carl, yeah. I wouldn't have wanted to see him like that; getting away with it; with all his friends patting his shoulder and comforting him." It figures that outside of depression, anger is the first emotion that rears.

"We could have asked him outright what happened then and there, and maybe saved ourselves the trip." I try to suppress that bit of my personality that wants to laugh and be proud of her. Hell, if she was shaking this all off, I would. But she isn't, because she's not like me. "Mind, it was Paul's idea to just go do the obvious thing, and I doubt we'd have gotten an admission out of him like you did."

Okay, that might have been a bit light if her glare is anything to go by. "That's not funny."

I shrug, looking back at the grave. "Wasn't meant to be. None of it's funny." A playful grimace. "Well, in retrospect, that whole thing with Ram might just have been. A little."

That doesn't lighten the tone as much as I'd

hoped it would, but maybe there's only so much humour that I can milk out of that particular ordeal. I play the card in my free hand as we stand there in silence, beginning to feel a bit stupid.

"I don't regret it, you know?" Tilley squints up at me, pale in the grey light. I can see every tiny dark pore in her pretty face. "Going round with you, I mean. I figured it was just going to be a laugh like every other time, but it was more…" She shakes her head, looks at the ground. I'd give her anything to finish that sentence. "It's good we did it together though."

Silence, and I can't tell if it's comfortable or obscene. My gut is twisting and alive with that same sick, giddy anticipation I used to get sneaking into a cinema through the fire escape. I don't know what the part of me existing a little in the future is so excited about though, and I elect to address the moment.

"Still, next time I pick up a possible murder investigation or a debauched enquiry, I'll leave you out of it."

"Oh hell no," she barks, snapping her eyes up to mind. "This is what life's about. I don't ever want to go that far again, but I need to see this stuff. Know what's really going on in the world." The words are halting as she absorbs the thing she's approaching with caution.

I regard her so seriously that I hardly know myself. "It's dangerous. I should know."

She smiles, warm and sure. "You'd look after me, just like I've looked after you and made sure you didn't kill yourself with a potato or something." The glint that's been missing since Thailand reignites as I watch.

"Your confidence in my self-preservation warms

my shrivelled black heart."

She reaches up on her toes and kisses me

I hold my breath and don't blink until she smirks at me and squeezes my hand, looking away.

Poor traumatised girl.

Doesn't know what she's doing.

I like it though.

Chapter 22

Swing

When we got back on home soil, I called Hugh to tell him what I'd found out. He invited Tilley and I over to his place the following evening to a shindig he was hosting. I was apprehensive. The last time I went to one of his parties, I ended up on a dirt bike trying to snap bull testicles off a line with my teeth. He'd called that one a hootenanny for some coke-fuelled reason. I hadn't seen any folk singers there, at any rate.

Still, we thought it might be good for us to get on with the normal stuff. Tilley drove us out into the desert, chattering like a chipmunk and smiling through the halo of smoke that crawled perpetually out of my mouth. We'd done a lot of talking on the plane and then carried on back at my flat. She stayed over and I didn't sleep in a dirty nest on the sofa. It was nice, though a bit weird.

As she calmed though, my own calm started to creep away until I felt like a blunt piece of flint. My journal hadn't been opened since Bangkok and I hadn't written a word. When my agent inevitably phoned, I took it into the bathroom and pissed into the receiver. I figured he'd get the message. I had more important things to do than write him a book, which was a blinding first.

After we park next to all the pick-ups and cars out front, we walk round to the back where the suspension party was taking place. Hugh's back 'garden' is as long and wide as he can be bothered to wander, so no one's lacking in space.

Skeletal wooden and metal rigs have been built, glowing orange from the many small fires that are going in the dirt. Nearest to the house, the frames are wound with white and blue fairy lights, and it's on one of those that the angels have set up.

Tilley and I got beers and sat touching shoulder to ankle on a flattened oil drum, watching the girls sway. Their shoulder blades had been play-pierced with long white feathers to give stunted wings that leaked blood. The long hooks that slung deep through their flesh projected just above the wings, five in all that ran up to a bar of metal and finally to the glowing frame itself. Strung up on metal wire by their skin, the angels laugh at the group watching and stroke at each other's sheer white dresses. Off to our left, a guy's adopted the lotus position five feet above the ground and has fallen into a meditative state, hanging by the flesh of his knees and back. To our right, a guy is just swinging and throwing empty beer cans.

It's going well until one of the angels announces that she's going to perform some poetry, inspired by the suspensions. I don't mind poetry, much to most people's astonishment, but I do mind that kind of arrogant lilt, and how she tips her head just so to look down the line of her nose at everyone. "I'm going to perform some poetry." The wrong stress grates. *PO*etry: gasp and faint at the honour. *PO*etry: kneel before me and bask in my select and haltingly delivered words. *PO*etry: bottle my breaths and snort it later like an elitist elixir. *PO*etry: bow and scrape you fucks, you commoners, you uneducated yobs who couldn't possibly appreciate the full blow and beauty of my gorgeous, masturbation-worthy words.

Tilley nudges me. "What's wrong?"

The remains of my beer don't ease the heat in my gut that's prickled outwards into my limbs and put a serrated line up my throat. I run a hand down her back for her to stay and stand, ploughing into the house away from the flying cow's sweaty POetry.

I'm instantly assaulted by the flat, thundering sound of a dozen paddles, palms and floggers impacting onto flesh over and over again, backed by barked laughs, orders and a few sinewy moans. Outside everyone is flying from steel hooks, but in here it's far baser. A full blown play-party.

I see Nora strapped up on a Saint Andrew's cross, her bare breasts lashed red and saliva dripping in long ropes from her bit gag. Hugh is flying thin strips of rubber into her from two neon floggers. His face is composed, serious. I can't see the sex dolls he uses for a sofa anywhere. Someone slaps my arms and it feels like a child. I keep walking. Everything is turned up to the same volume and words are getting distorted. 'Which one do you want?' 'Spread your legs and hold it.' 'Stop: red.' 'Not that one, that's mummy's favourite crop.' 'Boy or girl?'

On the car bonnet without knowing how I got there, I'm chain smoking my second cigarette and pulling out a third when Tilley arrives next to me. "Seriously Gabe, what's wrong?"

I want her to stop looking at me like that. It'll make me tell her. I swear, throw the cigarette down and light the fresh one. She waits me out in silence and eventually I talk to the ground. "The shit we saw in Thailand, Tilley. Fuck, I've seen some messed up, horrific lunatic shit in my time, but it's never stuck around in my head like this before."

There's nothing for a moment then she nods at me once. I have to take the invitation.

"I've been all over the fucking world these last few weeks, and I've seen all kinds of weird shit, and my limits of gross outrage have been massively extended. But do you know what I've found? All of it—kinky sex, beating your wife, strap-on anal sex, pissing about with genders—it all comes down to one very simple thing: adult informed consent. The whole world can fall into a straight-from-the-apocalypse orgy and I wouldn't give a shit as long as that line wasn't crossed."

God help me, I keep ranting.

"I've seen girls tortured for contraception, and men who cook other men from rival tribes to eat them. I've seen the worst piles you can imagine out of a guy's arse after he got fucked with a dildo run by an electric motor. And I've studied all that. I've asked question and taken interviews, then made a living out of it with a clean conscience. That's been my life, and the first time I don't ask the questions and write the book, because this time it's personal and really means something, then it just won't leave me alone." I stood up at some point, and now I'm breathing hard and looking down at Tilley on the car. "So what the hell does that make me?"

She tips her head, silent and still and calmer than I've ever seen. I have to refuse her hand when it reaches for mine, until I know what she's thinking.

"I don't think all that makes you a bad person. What kind of hypocrite would I be now if I said it did?" I'm shaking and it gets worse when I finally let her hold my hand. "You're just equipped for this stuff. To see it, to try to understand it and to write books about it."

My blood evaporates and leaves behind red lead.

"You know about the books?"

A smirk and her strangely sweet condescending look. "I'm not stupid. I've got all your books. It's not like I believed you were just working in different countries when you fell out of touch." Her expression fades into something more serious and queerly warm. "But what I'm getting at is that it's good it bothers you. It means you do have a conscience in there." She squeezes my hand. "And maybe you just need someone to go with you on your research trips in the future to remind you of that."

I sit back down, dumbfounded. Tilley remains composed, superiorly assured. "You're sure? It's awful sometimes, and after everything with Ben, are you sure you'd want—"

She shuts me up with a kiss. I don't care how often she disagrees with me as long as she stops all my protests like this. "You need to write this stuff because it shouldn't be written, and I'm going to make sure you're okay with it. Shit happens sometimes. We'll just suck up and move on. Besides, not all of it'll be awful. Some of it will just be weird and hilarious. Like old times."

I let go of her hand and put my arm around her, pulling her head under my chin and kissing her hair. "Cheers, Tilley."

She pokes me in the ribs. "If we could do all the overseas travelling by boat though, that'd be grand."

"Anything you want."

About the Author

KJ Moore does not believe in having matching furniture, E-Readers or "enough" DVDs.

Made in the USA
Monee, IL
12 May 2023